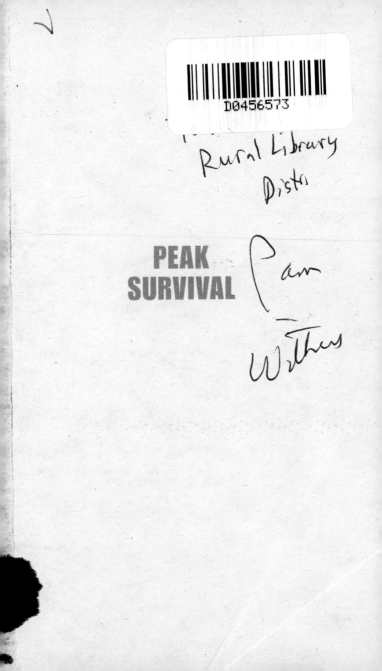

**PEAK
SURVIVAL**

Pam

Withers

PEAK SURVIVAL

Pam Withers

Dedicated with love to my ever-adventurous parents,
Richard and Anita Miller

Text copyright © 2004 by Pam Withers
Walrus Books, an imprint of Whitecap Books
Fourth printing, 2006

Edited by Carolyn Bateman
Proofread by Elizabeth McLean
Cover and interior design by Roberta Batchelor
Cover photograph by Digital Vision @ GettyImages
Printed and bound in Canada

National Library of Canada Cataloguing in Publication Data

Withers, Pam
 Peak survival / Pam Withers.

 (Take it to the extreme)
 ISBN 1-55285-530-9

 1. Skis and skiing—Juvenile fiction. 2. Snowboarding—Juvenile fiction
I. Title. II. Series: Withers, Pam. Take it to the extreme.
PS8595.I8453R42 2004   JC813'.6   C2003-907111-1

The publisher acknowledges the support of the Canada Council for
the Arts and the Cultural Services Branch of the Government of British
Columbia for our publishing program. We acknowledge the financial
support of the Government of Canada through the Book Publishing
Industry Development Program for our publishing activities.

We are committed to protecting the environment and to the responsible use of natural
resources. We are acting on this commitment by working with suppliers and printers to phase
out our use of paper produced from ancient forests. This book is printed by Webcom on 100%
recycled (40% post-consumer) paper, processed chlorine free and printed with vegetable-based
inks. We are working with Markets Initiative (www.oldgrowthfree.com) on this project.

Contents

1	The Heliport	1
2	Liftoff	9
3	Debris	19
4	Shelter	38
5	Sleepover	55
6	Midnight Chat	63
7	The Plane	70
8	Window and Stairs	83
9	Freedom	92
10	Action	102
11	Visitors	111
12	Steep and Gnarly	117
13	Ghost Town	128
14	Wheels	136
15	Yellow Ribbons	150
	Acknowledgements	154
	About the Author	170

1   The Heliport

The moment the van marked "Sam's Adventure Tours" pulled into the helicopter quarters' icy driveway, Jake Evans and Peter Montpetit lunged for the door and leaped to the ground.

"Race you to the chopper!" Peter shouted as he slid toward the launch pad, blond curls bobbing from beneath his colorful ski cap, designer sunglasses bouncing from the strap around his neck.

Jake shrugged, smiled, and broke into a fast walk. He knew his hyped-up friend would win the sprint. For Peter, every moment was a do-or-die competition.

"I reached it first," Peter shouted, lifting a gloved finger to carve his initials in the snow on the helicopter's window.

Jake stood on the tips of his toes and grinned. "Yeah, well, I'm the first to touch the chopper blades." He was about to run a glove reverently along the length of one when he remembered getting in trouble for doing so before. He shivered as wind billowed through his baggy jeans and tousled his unruly brown hair.

"Holy torpedo, look at the size of her," Peter exclaimed. "I may be a pilot's kid, but I've never seen one of *these* beasts close up, never climbed inside one. Can you believe how lucky we are? Just a couple of hours and it'll lift us off to a Canadian peak and leave us to schuss through paradise. What a way to spend spring break! You on skis, me on my new snowboard. What awesome jobs we have, Jake old buddy."

"A *potential* job I got you, which you're still trying out for," Jake teased. "I'm the junior heli-ski guide; you're the board-guide trainee. Better do what I command or Nancy won't promote you."

"Hey, I heard that," said Nancy Sheppard as she and Sam Miller caught up with their fleet-footed employees. Their tall, slim manager and her stocky, red-bearded boss were smiling. "At fifteen, you're still both trainees as far as I'm concerned, at least till you help us unload the van and check in with Joe."

"Who?" Peter asked.

"Joe Wilson is our pilot — you know, your friend Moses' dad," Sam replied as he pulled some forms from a worn leather satchel.

"Moses' dad, from the Indian reservation up north?"

"It's 'reserve,' not 'reservation' in Canada, Peter, remember? Yes, Joe's helicopter business in Prince George has gotten so big that he and his cousin have opened a second office down here in Mt. Currie to catch the Whistler ski and board crowd. You drove through Whistler just twenty-five minutes ago. Anyway, come on, guys. Back to the van, then into the office. Lots of work to do before you get that big brunch you've been going on about the entire ride up from Vancouver."

Jake stepped down from the helipad, Peter at his heels. They slogged back to the parking lot and began ferrying skis, poles, a snowboard, and packs from the van into the helicopter office, which consisted of a one-room, corrugated-tin-roofed building with one window, beside the helipad. Outside, a red and white neon sign dwarfed the entire structure. "Eagle Heli-Ski Tours, Mt. Currie, British Columbia," Jake read, admiring the smart-looking native graphic resembling an eagle.

"Good morning, Jake and Peter. Long time no see!" Joe Wilson rose from his office chair behind a counter as they stepped through the doorway. "In fact, I reckon you've each shot up an inch since last summer. Bet you've grown some muscles, too."

"Hi, Mr. Wilson," Jake responded with a broad smile. "Is Moses here yet? He's been e-mailing me every day for weeks, he's so excited about joining us."

Joe opened a closet door, pulled out a heavy parka, and stuffed his long arms into it as Nancy and Sam stepped inside. "He's down at the café, probably working his way through the entire supply of sticky cinnamon buns there, so better get yourself organized and join him. I'll help you load. It's 10:30. We leave in two and a half hours."

"That's assuming the weather stays perfect, right?" Nancy asked the pilot, glancing out the window. Jake followed her eyes. Looked good to him: clear blue sky.

"Regardless of what the morning brings," said Joe. "You leave weather worries to me. After twenty years in this business, I know just what my machines can handle."

"Agreed. Hey, I hear you've got a competitor across the road," Sam said as he exchanged some forms with Joe and signed them on the counter.

"Kids," Joe replied with a frown.

Jake, balancing a large load of gear, paused on his way out the door toward the four-passenger 206. He had to strain his ears to hear Joe's next comments: "Two young lads are running it on an uncle's invest-ment, their first business. Seem to think their name — 'Extreme Adventure Tours' — is so special that clients will rush over to do business with them. I'd be surprised if they make it through the season."

He reached the 'copter, yanked its door open, and smiled as Jake and Peter leaped in.

"After we stow this stuff, can I sit in the driver's seat?" Peter asked, reaching for the controls and running his hand along the smooth upholstery. Jake half expected him to start bouncing on the seats.

"Not a chance," Joe laughed, "or there will be a severe cinnamon bun shortage at the café, as I warned you."

A short while later, the boys pushed open the door of the small café down the road. Jake instantly loved the old-fashioned, small-town feel of the place.

"How quaint," Peter said. "A real roadside diner. Get a load of those red stools along the counter. I bet they spin."

"I'll spin this saucer straight atcha if you let go any more remarks," boomed a voice from a booth a short distance away. Jake turned to see Moses Wilson rise and approach them with a big grin on his pudgy face, hands on his hips, baseball cap tilted on his cropped black hair.

"Moses! Great to see you!" Jake said, slapping the husky boy on his broad back as Peter smiled and pressed a friendly knuckle into his shoulder. "So we're going to show how it's done up on the slopes, eh? Isn't it awesome that Sam's Adventure Tours hired your dad for this trip? — 'cause I get to work with you!

And Nancy says after this overnight training trip, Peter might be ready to come with us on a few end-of-season weekend client trips. When he can get up here from Seattle, that is."

"No worries," Moses responded, his face glowing. "You'n me'll show this visiting Yank what Lillooet Glacier powder is all about. Maybe get him a promotion, you think, even if he is on a board?"

"It's a deal, fellow pilot's kid," Peter laughed. "Soon as we get the full, deluxe-version, heli-adventurers' breakfast into our withered stomachs. Can't shoot the slopes on nothing, that's for sure. I've been starved since my bus pulled out of Seattle last night. Got into Vancouver at midnight, ate stale pizza at my cousin's place before we crashed."

"Yeah, well, Sam and Nancy and I left Chilliwack an hour and a half before we even picked you up in Vancouver, so we're the hungry ones," Jake replied.

As the boys slid into the booth, the jingle of a bell on the café's door signaled a new arrival. Expecting Nancy and Sam, Jake looked up to see a well-heeled couple with a tall, slim daughter about the same age as the boys. The girl gave the boys a fleeting glance before turning her back on them.

Peter let go a low whistle as she shook a head of red hair from her ski cap, hung her fancy red ski jacket over her mother's expensive leather one on the café's wobbly coat rack, and slid into a booth out of view.

"I say we ride in her helicopter," Peter suggested, prompting Jake to roll his eyes.

"No can do. She's flying with the competition, poor thing," Moses whispered. "Saw her checking in over there with a very expensive-looking snowboard. I guess she's on her way to doing something *extreme*."

"I say she's extremely hot," Peter sneered, "and your competition seems to have higher-class customers."

"We were doing alright till folks like you drove down our prospects," Moses teased back.

"Well, I say she's stuck up, and who cares?" Jake offered. "What's important is giving our helicopter some ballast — if we can get that waitress to notice us."

"Yeah," Peter agreed, swiping a cinnamon bun from Moses' plate before Moses could react.

It was late morning by the time Jake, Peter, Moses, Nancy, and Sam filed back through the Eagle Heli-Ski Tours door. As they finished loading gear into the special basket that ran the length of the 'copter's right side, Jake glanced at the late-March sky: still blue as the ocean except for a few stratus clouds moving like a flock of gulls in a hurry. Good, Jake thought, stuffing his hands deeper into the pockets of the ski pants he'd just donned. Even after a year of serving as lowly odd-job boy, cook, and sometime junior guide at Sam's Adventure Tours, he always felt a little nervous at the start of a new adventure, even a training trip without paying clients to look after, like this one. It's not that he doubted his skiing abilities – he'd grown very slick at backcountry skiing over the past winter – or even that he was worried about the cold tonight, when Nancy, Sam, he, and the other boys bedded down in winter sleeping bags and a sturdy tent on the slopes. No, he loved outdoor adventures of all kinds and was thrilled that Sam and Nancy were allowing Peter, Moses, and him to take this trip together.

It's just that, well, it was a big deal to step out of a helicopter ten thousand feet up a mountain, attach skis or a snowboard to your feet, hoist a pack on your back, and confront a hundred miles of remote backcountry stretching in almost every direction. Even though all the boys had been trained in avalanche dangers, backcountry first aid, and wilderness survival, Jake wondered, could they really handle it?

He sighed. When would he ever learn to stop worrying? He was outfitted with the best gear and training the company could offer, he was as strong and fit as he'd ever been, and Sam and Nancy would be with them every step of the way. Time to relax and enjoy himself, like his impulsive and ever energetic friend from south of the border.

2　Liftoff

"Who gets to sit up front?" Jake asked Joe, pressing his palms together in praying fashion.

"Moses is my man," the owner replied, proudly locking a mitt on his son's shoulder. "You and Nancy can sit in back."

Jake's shoulders slumped, but he figured there was no use arguing.

"Jake and Nancy?" Peter cried in dismay. "But there're only two seats in back, and Jake and I want to fly together."

Jake elbowed Peter and signaled him to lower his shrill voice. Peter coughed and tried again in a quieter tone. "We *must* fly together, Mr. Wilson. He's training me for a junior guide position."

"And then where would your adult supervision be for the two hours it takes me to return with your bosses?"

"Adult supervision?" Peter pressed. "Jake and Moses have been guiding skiers on weekends all season — and looking forward to finally guiding together this weekend — and you know I'm a strong snowboarder. Please, Mr. Wilson, didn't Jake and I kayak ninety-five miles of horrendous whitewater river rapids — *alone* — to save that stranded rafting party last year? If you can't trust us alone for two hours, there's no point calling us junior guides."

"Or junior guide trainees," Nancy cut in, as she hauled the last of the gear to the 'copter. "Joe, he's got a point. Sam and I will wait for the second trip as long as these three adventurers promise *on pain of being fired* not to do anything foolish after you drop them off."

Jake held out his open palm for Peter to high-five.

"They can set up the tent and have our soup ready," Sam suggested.

"Promise!" Jake enthused, echoed by Moses and Peter in chorus.

Joe frowned, studied the skidding line of clouds, and looked as if he was about to object when a smiling Moses clapped his gloved hand over his father's mouth and led the tall man to the helicopter. Jake felt Peter grip his shoulder in quiet victory. He turned to see Nancy studiously ignoring that. She lifted his backpack, allowing him to climb into the helicopter.

"See you in 120 minutes," she said, her dark eyes stern as the boys placed the bulky loads on their laps. "Jake, you do have the radio, right? And it's time for all of us to turn on our transmitters. Those," she reminded Peter, "are transmitter beacons that help us locate one another in the event of an avalanche."

"Aye, aye, Captain, I know," Peter responded with a salute. Everyone pressed the buttons that activated the transmitters hanging around their necks.

What nerve Peter has to talk to Nancy like that, thought Jake. Doesn't he get that she's his boss, and a strict one, too? He fastened the elaborate lap and shoulder belt that made him feel like a toddler in a car seat and gave both Nancy and Sam what he hoped was a reassuring smile.

"Time to put on your headphones," Joe directed, jabbing a finger at the equipment beside the boys. Jake hated how the heavy, static-filled sets were the only way to communicate inside the helicopter once it started up, but he had become used to it over the course of the past winter's training. As Jake pulled on the aluminum and plastic earmuffs, any concerns starting to sprout in his mind were soon drowned out by the loud clattering of the rotors overhead and the tingle of excitement he always felt at takeoff. Despite a near-complete season of weekend heli-ski guiding for Sam's Adventure Tours, Jake still thrilled to the effortless liftoff of the glass globe whose belly offered a 360-degree view of the world. He loved the way the helicopter whipped up a small snowstorm below its hovering skids, forcing Sam and Nancy to back up and pull their parka hoods around their faces. Were they worried? Jake wondered as he returned their waves. Should they really have let the boys go on ahead?

"Wipe that serious expression off your face," a voice crackled into his earphones. Jake looked up to see Moses twisted around to grin at him. "Perk up, Jake. We've been waiting forever for this overnight — and no clients to worry about. Now that the peak season's over, we get to help train next season's slave labor. Think Peter knows what he's in for?"

"I'm in for a perfect weekend of backcountry free-riding on my cool new board," retorted Peter. "And if you guys pitch the tent and make the meals, I might even show you some hot new moves. I've decided to be boss up here, by the way. I've got years of experience over either of you. Been skiing and boarding since almost before I was born."

"Yeah, but mostly on groomed slopes," Jake said. Ever jealous of Peter's fearlessness and skills on the slope, he felt like adding, "And you don't have an ounce of sense to show for it," but he held his tongue. No point starting a trip off on the wrong foot, and Peter had only been joking.

"Delusional as always, Peter," came Moses' dry response.

"Sam and Nancy are the only bosses needed," Joe inserted.

As if to squelch further discussion, the gently hovering craft took off diagonally, like a gondola rising on an invisible cable headed toward the array of peaks that stretched away northwest to Monmouth Mountain above Lillooet Glacier.

"Moose at ten o'clock," Joe shouted into the system a short while later. The boys strained to see where a clock's little hand would be pointing to ten, had the bright white scene below them been a clock face. There they saw a slow-moving black speck just below treeline as the helicopter climbed higher.

"Cool!" enthused Peter. "What other wildlife have we got up here?"

"Bobcats, wolves, wolverines, and rabbits," Moses replied. "Bears, but they're still hibernating. Porcupines and elk farther down the valley. And whisky-jacks that will land on your hand for bread crumbs."

"Mmmm, wolverine and whisky-jack pie when we get super hungry," said Peter.

Jake smiled. Could Peter ever think of anything besides food?

"Never seen a wolverine in all my years up here, and you couldn't eat one even if you managed to kill it before it killed you," Joe returned. "They'd probably make shoe leather taste tender."

"The weather is turning more unsettled," Jake broke in. "Never seen clouds move so fast."

"Means violent winds up high," Joe allowed, without elaboration or a note of concern, but Jake noticed him eye a black cloud on the far southwest horizon that had appeared from nowhere.

"Dad was a helicopter jockey in the Vietnam war."

"Vietnam war? But he's Canadian," Peter said.

"You didn't know that some Canadians signed up for the action?" Moses responded. "He can fly in pretty much anything, right Dad?"

"Mmmm," Joe replied.

In what seemed far less than a forty-minute tour of spectacular mountain vistas, Jake felt the helicopter slow. He peered out as it hung decisively over a neat shelf near the top of one of the highest windswept peaks. He held his breath as Joe maneuvered his bird to sit gracefully on the ledge and cut the throttle.

"Ten thousand feet in altitude, and my guess is about ten feet of snow," Joe announced as Jake lifted his hands to his earphones. He watched Peter squirm with impatience for the helicopter to stop vibrating. Jake's ears were still ringing as he lifted off the earphones, opened the door, and leaped into the blowing snow. He cursed as his radio slipped from his pocket, bounced on the doorsill, and dropped into the snow. He stooped to pick it up and put it back in his pocket. Arms hugging his heavy pack, face stinging from the unexpected cold, Jake made his way around to the basket that held the skis. He dropped his pack in the soft snow, braced as gusts of wind hammered him, and breathed deeply of the cold, fresh air. So fresh, his teeth ached. He grabbed his skis and poles. When Moses and Peter had their gear in hand, Jake, like his buddies, backed away, ducked, and waved at Joe, who leaned out his window to shout, "On pain of being fired, no foolishness …"

They smiled, bobbed their heads like nodding-dog toys stuck on a car dashboard, and crouched as the helicopter roared to life again. It lifted away to leave them in sudden silence pierced by the shrill wind.

"Awesome place," Peter enthused. "How about a quick slide down to that kicker to stretch our muscles after the ride? No harm in that as long as we get the tent set up straightaway afterwards, right? Best place for it down there anyway."

Jake hesitated, sizing up the fall line — the steepest route — between them and where Peter was pointing. He cast a sideways glance at Moses, who met his eyes, shrugged, and smiled.

"If we're careful," Jake decided.

"Race you there," Peter replied, pulling on his goggles and stuffing his boots into his bindings.

"No, we're going to stay in the position I tell you: me first, you second, and Moses last," Jake ordered. Before Peter could protest, Jake clicked his boots into his bindings and took off.

Jake, mindful that the least experienced person was always supposed to be in the middle, knew Peter would never admit to being the least experienced, and in many ways, he might be the best in a technical sense. But when it came to mountain rescue training and local knowledge of these mountains, Moses and Jake had a leg up — especially Moses, whose family had spent generations trapping in the valleys to the northeast. Anyway, Jake and Moses had completed Sam's Adventure Tours guide training, which included backcountry safety, and Peter was only halfway through. In any case, Peter might not immediately catch onto the fact that they'd placed him in the middle for a reason.

Jake's heart thudded against his rib cage a bit as he fought away thoughts of what Nancy would say if she knew they were about to play before setting up the tent. But there was plenty of time to erect their dome before she and Sam arrived. And she hadn't said they couldn't ski or board. She'd just warned them not to do anything foolish. He'd make sure no one did.

Jake turned to check that everyone behind him was

fine, then sped up. He couldn't help but savor the thrill of wind whistling past his ears, and the smooth glide of his skis through virgin powder. Unlike commercial ski hills, where packed snow and slow skiers forced him to hold back, putting tracks in fresh powder made him feel like an Olympian, or a sculptor handed master tools to create whatever he liked. He poured his heart and every muscle of his well-toned body into drawing curves through the untouched powder. Straight down the fall line, hands forward, skis in parallel, poetry in motion. He couldn't fathom a more wondrous sense of freedom, raw wind pushing against his taut form, every muscle on fire as he breathed life into the mountain by tracing wiggly veins down her body. Moses and Peter, too, were grinning as they raced down the brilliant white slope. As he reached the snowy plateau, however, Jake signaled that it was time to stop.

"Aw, just a few more minutes," Peter pleaded.

"On pain of …" Jake started to quote Nancy.

"The mother of all thunderclouds is on her way over here," Moses interrupted. Jake swung around. Moses was right. Where there had been only blue sky just two hours before, now the bowl just over their heads was turning heavy and gray, with a defined bank of black moving from the southwest like a freight train.

"Let's get camp set up …" Jake started to say, when the sound of an approaching chopper threatened to drown out his words.

"An A-Star," Moses shouted. "That would be Extreme Adventures, come to be our neighbors up here, too." The three boys shaded their eyes as the small chopper slowed and hung near a rock cliff on the mountaintop opposite them, half a mile away as an eagle flies. They were all still staring at the helicopter when it whipped up a snow cloud from which emanated a sudden, sickening sound of metal screeching against rock. Why was the pilot trying to land so close to the rock cliff? Jake thought, his stomach churning. They watched, eyes wide, as rotating blades crumpled against the rock cliff, causing the machine to spool down and begin a gut-wrenching tumble down the slope. Parts flew off in every direction, and Jake thought he heard the bubble crack just before it came to a precarious stop a hundred feet below its intended landing spot. The snow whipped up by the landing must have blinded the pilot to how close he was to it. Even from their distant perch, Jake was sure he could detect burning wire, and the smell made him suddenly nauseous. Then, as quickly as the mountaintop silence had been broken, it resumed with an unbearable heaviness, disturbed only by the moans of the wind.

3   Debris

Time froze for several terrible minutes as Peter, Jake, and Moses stared at the remnants of the helicopter across the gully. Peter was the first to spring to action.

"Could be survivors!" he shouted, grabbing his backpack and clipping his boots into his snowboard. As he fitted on his goggles, thoughts of changing cloud patterns and promises made vanished from his mind. Then he felt Jake's arm clamp down on his shoulder.

"We need to call Mr. Wilson first," Jake declared, pulling out his radio. "He's still in the air. He can come back, get those people to hospital. And we need to figure out the safest route. We need to keep separated on the way over there. That way, if anyone sets off a small slide, the others have time to change course." He gripped the transmitter around his neck. Peter bristled under Jake's menacing glare, but as he opened his mouth to speak, Jake finished, "And I'm going first."

Peter felt his face grow hot. How dare Jake take over! How dare he anoint himself first one down again! How dare he waste precious seconds when people might be dying. Let Jake radio while he and Moses headed over.

But once again, Jake cut him off, this time by spinning away from him, radio pressed to his ear. Peter looked at Moses, who stood silently, refusing to take his eyes off the downed helicopter, or maybe refusing to take sides. But after a few seconds' silence, Moses donned his pack and skis, and turned to Peter.

"Cut left, run down that cut over there, then traverse to the right. Should be a straight shot from there," his deep voice directed. "Shouldn't take us more than twenty minutes to get there. Keeping distance between us is important, Peter. The crash may have destabilized that slope, and if one of us starts a slide, we don't want anyone caught in its path."

Peter grunted. At least Moses hadn't said, "Jake is right about keeping distance between us." Of course they had to do that. Didn't even need to be said, right? Peter rocked in place on his board and twisted his head back and forth to see whether Jake was ready yet, or whether Moses seemed willing to head out before Jake gave the word. Lives were at stake here, and

Peter's stomach was totally cramped from what they'd just witnessed. They needed to go.

"Can't get through," Jake finally said, face grim as he lowered the radio. "Maybe it got damaged when it dropped out of the helicopter."

"We'll try again from down there. Let's go," Moses said.

That's all Peter needed to shoot away like a starting gun had gone off. He cruised down the route Moses had suggested for a full minute before glancing back to see Moses following, and Jake still putting on his skis.

"That'll teach him," Peter thought, speeding up to assert his lead. But his mind was more on the debris spilled over the mountain ahead. His gut felt like a twisted rope. His breathing was coming hard, and not from the snowboarding or the altitude. His eyes kept scanning, scanning the dark pieces scattered in the pristine snow below the crash site. How could this have happened? What were the chances of everyone — or even anyone — in that helicopter being okay? What should he do first when he got to the scene? Would he be able to remember stuff from Nancy's first-aid training? What if the slope started to give out from under them as they searched for survivors? And what if he, Jake, and Moses had been in that helicopter?

His mind was racing faster than his board. The wind

was pummeling his body. His throat felt very, very dry. He had to stop looking at the accident site, had to focus on the snow beneath him. Had to get there safely. Had to show Jake and Moses the best way. Moses was right; the traverse was a good plan. He shifted his back foot, bent his knees, and leaned forward until his face seemed inches from the surface of the powder. The board whipped around, throwing up a rooster tail of snow. He raced at full speed toward the bubble.

Normally, he'd have been proud of pulling off such a sweet toe-side carve. But his mind and body were squeezed around just one thing at the moment: what he was about to confront.

Pieces of machinery glinted left, right, and center as he approached the helicopter. Then he spotted it: a body resting face-down in the snow. He knelt beside what resembled a parka tossed carelessly into a heap. It wasn't just a parka; he knew that as he reached toward the back of its hood. But it wasn't a conscious person, either. Not in that mangled, still position. His fingers hesitated as he touched the back of the hood. His stomach turned very, very tight.

"He might be alive," Peter whispered, steeling himself to lean over further and scoop out some snow from beneath the man's mouth. Maybe that would help him breathe? Peter removed his own glove, holding his bare hand near the man's mouth. He could feel no breath. He dared not turn the man over or lift his head. He knew that much from first aid. It could kill the man if he already had a neck or spine injury. Instead, he slid his shaking fingers along the man's throat to find his pulse. He knew where it should be. They'd practiced on dummies in first-aid class.

"Pretend he's the dummy in first-aid class," Peter ordered himself, squeezing his eyes shut for a moment. That helped. But only until his fingers felt something wet and sticky. He yanked them back and stared wide-eyed at the blood, then plunged them into the white snow to clean them.

Get a grip, he told himself. Find the pulse. Doesn't matter if he's bleeding. Is he alive?

He turned his pale face up to Moses, who had pulled up beside him. Jake was moving toward the bubble. Biting his tongue, Peter tried again. Nothing. Definitely nothing. No pulse.

"You try," he urged Moses, staggering away. Moses removed his gloves and tried, first on the man's throat, then on his wrists, then on his throat again. Face ashen, Moses moved his blood-soaked hand to the top of the hood and pulled it down gently. That's when both boys stumbled backward into the snow and Moses turned away to retch. Peter fought the same urge himself. They didn't need a doctor to tell them this was a corpse.

"He was so young!" Peter's mind shrieked. "Too young!"

"Moses! Peter! Help me!" Jake was calling. They were only too glad to scramble up and make for the bubble.

The helicopter had landed on one side, Peter noticed, and that side had had its door stripped off. That must have been the side the man they'd just left had been thrown from. Had he unbuckled his seat belt to try to jump out?

Jake was standing on top of the helicopter, trying to lift the other door open like a hatch, but the handle had been crushed during the roll down the slope. He removed his gloves to work his fingers under the crushed handle and tried again. Peter noted that two bodies were slumped inside, the pilot and someone in the back.

Peter leaped up to help Jake as Moses looked through the cracked windshield, hands cupped around his eyes. A terrific grating noise sounded as the door opened, tossing Jake and Peter into the snow. Peter was the first on his feet again, climbing up to check out the driver. Again, he could get no pulse. He turned his eyes away from the enormous bruise above the pilot's left eyebrow as the head sagged like a bowling ball in his arms. He shook his head solemnly. Moses — and this time Jake, too —

confirmed the lack of pulse before gently — just in case they were wrong — undoing the pilot's seat belt and easing him out so they could reach the third victim.

That's when Peter heard muffled crying.

"Someone's alive!" he screamed to the boys below him.

"Alive!" Moses echoed from his position in front of the window. "Saw her move!"

"It's okay," Peter heard himself say to the figure in the red coat as he mopped sweat from his face and dove down toward her. "We're here. We'll get you out. You're okay."

"Please," the girl whispered before he could touch her. She opened her eyes but didn't seem to be looking at him. Her eye sockets were unnaturally large and her breath came in short gasps.

"Easy now," Peter responded as he reached around her. "Let me undo your seat belt. You could be injured."

He heard Jake cursing outside. "Gotta get through! Why isn't it working?" Then he felt Jake climb up and dive halfway into the upturned helicopter. He reached around Peter for the radiophone on the dashboard.

"Dead! Broken!" he screeched, holding it up in pained disbelief. Peter nodded his head to offer sympathy and watched Jake slither back up and out the door.

Peter sank his fingertips into the girl's neck and

applied a little pressure, just like Nancy had taught them, watching the girl's eyes for a pained reaction. Their panic-stricken look never altered. He adjusted her coat to allow him to run his fingers down her spine. She didn't wince from that, either. He didn't like the sound of her breathing — you'd think she'd just emerged from underwater — but judged her safe to move. He crawled up to the open hatch, half-blocked by Jake's face peering down at him. Jake moved away long enough for Peter to pop his head up and look around.

"Jake, fetch me that broken helicopter blade over there; it's as close to a backboard as we're going to find up here." Barely had the words come out when he felt the shock of a hand close around his ankle, so tightly that it felt as if she was trying to bruise him. He lowered himself down and stared at her. She grabbed his left wrist with her other hand, like a drowning victim trying to keep from going down.

"Hey there," he said as gently as he could, placing a hand on her sweaty forehead. Her eyes were bulging from her face; he'd never seen such panic. He felt her forehead. It felt both cold and clammy, but his touch made her relax her grip a little. He saw her try to focus on his face. He bent down and unpried her first hand, held it for an awkward second. Her pale blue eyes locked on his as if she thought blinking might prevent her from being rescued.

Without bothering to unlock her other hand from his wrist, he moved behind her, placed his hands under her armpits, and lifted her up toward Jake, who was hanging down from above.

Together, they eased her up to the top of the helicopter and onto the six-foot-long piece of rotor Jake had salvaged from the nearby snow. The second her head and shoulders emerged from the bubble, she let go of Peter's wrist and began to breathe more evenly. Her eyes darted about as the boys laid her down on the broken rotor.

"No," she started to protest, but Peter pressed a firm hand on her shoulder and gave her a no-arguing look. Although he saw no bruises or bleeding, he was taking no chances.

He ducked back down into the helicopter and came up again with some rope. Jake, who was on the radio again, suddenly threw it with force into the snow. Moses frowned, retrieved it, and stuffed it into his parka pocket.

"Let's lash her down so we can lower her to the ground," Peter said.

Moses joined in helping them move the girl to the snow. Peter noticed that the wind had picked up. It whistled around the downed craft as blowing snow filled the creases of their parkas and faces.

The moment they set the girl down, Jake jumped

up and walked in circles around her, scanning the slopes and the sky as if searching for something. He lifted one hand to shield his eyes and, after a moment, pointed to a ridge in the opposite direction from which they had come.

"Let's haul everything over to that rock ledge."

"What? Why?" Peter sputtered.

"Good choice," Moses spoke up. "Looks more stable there. Not safe to stay here any longer than we have to."

"Says who?" Peter challenged, but Moses didn't reply, and Jake said only, "Peter, grab whatever useful stuff you find in this 'copter before it slides any farther down the slope. Then let's get the heck out of here."

"Hey, who put you in charge?" Peter shot back. "Anyway, we should head the other way, to where we got dropped off, where they're expecting us to be in one hour."

"Peter," Jake was speaking between gritted teeth, "Look at the sky. Look at the slope we came down to get here. Then look at the ridge Moses and I just agreed would be the safest place to be. We have this girl to carry before the storm lands."

Peter couldn't believe Jake was speaking to him like that. But one look at the sky convinced him that whatever they were going to do, they'd better do it quickly. There wasn't time to argue. So he did as he was told, and within fifteen minutes, the group of four — the girl still full-length on her blade — had collected itself on the rock slab.

Peter heaped a pile of items retrieved from the helicopter, including the girl's fancy pink snowboard, on one end of the rock, beside which the boys piled skis, packs, and Peter's board. Peter seated himself between the gear and the girl's stretcher. She lay with no expression, face drawn. Peter wondered what she was thinking, how he'd feel after such a horrifying experience. By now, the blowing snow was starting to cover some of the helicopter debris. It was also tingeing their eyelashes with white.

Jake plunked himself down on a mound a short distance from the group on the rock and checked his watch. "Three o'clock. Forty-five minutes before Joe will be back. It's exposed enough up here he'll probably find us, even if we're not in the right place. Shall we go back to get the, er, bodies?"

No one replied immediately. Peter pulled a sleeping bag out of his backpack to cover the red-haired girl, who hadn't said a word since they'd lain her on the rotor.

Several moments passed as the boys continued to catch their breath and scan the wreckage from their perch. Peter wondered about the risk of hauling the men's bodies to their rock. His eyes fastened on each of them, still visible across the expanse they'd just covered, like shadows on the snow. His stomach remained as clenched as when he'd first heard the crash. The red-haired girl finally broke the silence, startling them with a strong English accent.

"The fellow out of the helicopter was my guide. The other chap was the pilot. Both so young." She stopped. Peter peered at her, watched her chest heave and face contort with an effort to choke back tears. Peter couldn't imagine even bothering to battle tears after what she'd just been through. But after a moment, she continued. "My parents. What are they going to think when that helicopter doesn't return to Mt. Currie?"

Her lips tightened, her eyes squeezed shut. Tears streamed down her face at last. Still she made the effort to speak. "I'm not injured, you know. I don't know how, but I'm not. I'm going to sit up now."

"No!" Jake commanded, startling everyone.

The red-haired girl, still lying flat, spoke again.

"This was supposed to be a dream trip, a special fifteenth birthday present from my parents: a heli-snowboarding trip in British Columbia. We flew all the way from London, England, last week. Really, I'm okay. Let me sit up. Thank you for pulling me out."

Peter was torn between saying "you're welcome," which sounded stupid, and turning away as she broke into sobs. Finally, she stopped.

"My name is Fiona Kerton. We should organize all this gear, you know."

As she said this, the sleeping bag tucked around her flew off in a gust of wind. Peter gave chase and caught it. By the time he'd returned, Fiona's face had regained its color and composure. Had she really said something about organizing gear? Was this the same girl who'd bruised his ankle and hyperventilated till they'd removed her from the bubble? Still in shock, he supposed, but an unusual girl, chatting with them so soon after the ordeal. He couldn't imagine what state of mind he'd be in. He did know they couldn't let her move till someone had checked her over. Someone who'd finished advanced first-aid training. Why hadn't Jake or Moses volunteered?

Jake finally sighed, moved up to her stretcher, and knelt in the snow beside her, his eyes everywhere but on hers. Peter smiled inwardly. Jake was useless talking to girls at the best of times, and Fiona was definitely good-looking.

"My name's Jake Evans. I'm checking for injuries. I've passed wilderness first-aid training, so just cooperate. Okay?" Peter dared a glance at Fiona's face and wondered if he saw a hint of a smile. Moses crawled up to help Jake untie the rope holding Fiona as Peter looked on.

"Are you hurting anywhere?" Jake began.

"No," Fiona replied. Peter thought he must have imagined the smile. She was looking weary and pale again.

"Can you wriggle your toes?"

"Yes."

"No numbness?"

"No numbness."

Peter watched Jake's face start to redden. "I'm going to palpate your neck, then down your spine. Tell me if you feel any tenderness." He kneaded his hand lower and lower, clearly forcing himself to search her face. Peter wondered if he'd done the procedure right the first time. He hoped Jake wouldn't find something he hadn't.

"You're one very lucky passenger," Jake finally ruled. Slowly, stiffly, still pale, Fiona sat up. She creased the sleeping bag that had been lying across her and placed it neatly on the rock beside her as if folding a linen napkin at the close of a dinner in a fine restaurant. She removed her handknit hat. Fire-red hair fell over strong shoulders, all the way to the small of her back. A few strands blew forward to her knees, which she drew up to her quivering chin as she rested her feet, clad in expensive-looking snowboard boots, on the rock shelf. Again, an awkward silence reigned as the boys waited for her to pull herself together.

"Thank you, Jake. I guess you had to make sure. It was the right thing to do. My father's a doctor, and

I'm going to be one, so I shouldn't have insisted I was okay before you did that."

Peter watched her shiver, clamp her hat on her head, and survey Moses and him; both had been staring at her since Jake had begun his procedure. Peter tried hard to think of something to say, was about to suggest they move now to fetch the bodies, when Fiona spoke again.

"Dare I ask if you fellows have radioed for help or something? You're not up here alone, are you? Especially with the weather picking up like this?"

Peter peered up. The picture sure wasn't pretty. The mother of all freight trains had all but taken over the sky while the boys had been intent on their search and rescue operation. Peter checked his watch: "Jake has been trying to radio, but it's not working. Half an hour till Moses' dad returns. He'll fly through this weather, right?"

As if in answer, Jake leaped up, grabbed the radio from Moses' pocket, and moved a short distance away, holding it to his ear. Like privacy mattered, Peter thought, or like it was going to start working suddenly. Just then, a horrific crack sounded from somewhere above.

At first, Jake assumed it was a thunderclap; then he wondered if it was another helicopter crash. But before he could ponder further, the world gave way beneath him. He felt himself falling down a chute, like the "black hole" tube at his favorite waterslide park, except that instead of a wet thrill, it offered cold terror. He felt helpless to fight the plunge, but from somewhere deep within his instincts came an order to "swim." He tried the front crawl. No good. His nostrils were filling with snow, and a panic to breathe gripped him. He switched to breaststroke, knowing it wasn't going to save him from this avalanche, but it was something to do as the snow swept him to his death. Would his head snap half off like Fiona's guide? Or would he hit a piece of churning helicopter wreckage and black out with only a bruise on his face to show for it, like the pilot? Or would the avalanche leave him buried so deep that he would slowly suffocate as his buddies searched from above? Or were all four of them being tossed and spun like planks in a rogue surf wave? Reaching for the light in his blurry snow prison, he swam with all his strength toward it, but he remained a drowning victim spinning within sight of the surface, deprived of the oxygen it promised. As the ride began to slow, he struggled to pull his hands to his face, cupping them just beyond his mouth to make airspace.

Breathe slowly, he told himself. You're a diver with a small tank of oxygen. Don't do anything to speed up its loss. Finally, the falling sensation ended. He felt suspended in white nothingness, which was neither dark nor light. If it's not dark, I have some hope of being near the surface, he thought. That helped him control the temptation to all-out panic. He tried to move his ski-boot-clad feet, but they seemed to be cast in concrete. He tried to move his elbows, head, hands, fingers, anything, but where only moments before the snow gods had allowed him to swim, they seemed to have since clamped shut the coffin lid. How could snow — those gentle flakes children use to make angels or snowmen, that powder that could make for such sweet skiing — become so deathly compacted? How could it trap a person who, only minutes before and god-knows how many miles above, had been standing near friends who were now — well, who knows where?

He couldn't move, but he could breathe, and as far as he could determine, he was still alive. How long the oxygen pack he'd formed with his cupped hands would last, he couldn't say for sure; it seemed impossible to track time in this position anyway. Best to think happy thoughts, thoughts that would suck minimum oxygen from his stash. Thoughts of his mother, or younger sister. Thoughts of his favorite sports, his best adventures. Maybe he should cut a deal with the mountain, tell her that if she let him out of here alive, he'd never get cross with his mother or sister again, never curse his father for disappearing a few years ago after a big fight with his mom, and then not writing or supporting them since. If ever the snow freed him, he'd take his mother and sister out to dinner somewhere in Chilliwack. And he would, he promised the avalanche, somehow, someday, find and forgive his father.

Voices. Female voices. His mother and sister? No, that would mean he was in the funeral parlor, and he hadn't been dug out of the snow yet and taken there, had he? He tried to shout, tried to kick, but it only made him break out in a sweat, made him feel bundled, tied, and gagged. Then he heard shouting, and the sound of shovels. Guys' voices, his buddies. Easy, boys, don't jam those shovels into my skull, please. And then his saviors loosed the snow from above his head, and Peter's face leaned down close to his, blinding daylight surrounding his blond curls like a halo.

"Jake? That you? Never thought I'd be so glad to see you in my life."

"Never thought I'd welcome your ugly face stuck right in my face either," Jake replied in short gasps. "I owe you."

"Nah, you owe Fiona, who put her beacon to

'receive,' picked up your signal, and cruised down here by snowboard to show us where to dig. But she owed us before that," Peter bantered as two shovels and one end of Fiona's snowboard continued to remove snow from around Jake's shoulders. He tried to adjust his eyes to the light.

Once he'd climbed out of his hole and been declared uninjured by Moses, Jake flushed as he was hugged by two of his three rescuers. Fiona stood back, eyes cast on her feet, leaning against the bright pink snowboard planted beside her. Though still blinking, he wondered how he could have imagined the daylight to be so brilliant. It was, in fact, getting dark, and the storm that had been brewing since the other helicopter had tried to set down was clearly on the verge of breaking. He had no idea if Joe would risk a return trip in these new conditions, but he did know that with all signs of the crashed helicopter erased by the avalanche, their radio gone from his hand, and frightening winds coming upon them, shelter was now top priority.

Moses was clearly thinking the same. He pointed sixty feet up the ridge. "The pile of gear Peter rescued from the helicopter is still on the rock ledge; so are our backpacks. You were the only one swept down. The rest of us had a balcony-seat view of the entire slide. How lucky was that? And unlucky for you ..."

4   Shelter

Peter clamped his and Moses' skis together and raised a pair to each shoulder as Moses kicked and shoveled the first foothold for them in the mountainside.

Six slanted stories above them, the rock ledge holding their gear beckoned: the ledge where they'd been seated when the sonic boom of the avalanche had sounded. Peter figured he could almost hit the gear with a snowball from where he stood, but climbing up there was going to be a major pain. The avalanche-churned snow was hard as concrete, and the slope resembled an upended field of giant broken boulders, any of which could start rumbling down again during the group's attempt to clamber up and over them. Peter eyed their backpacks still forming a neat pile atop the shelf and shuddered at the memory of how Jake had been whisked away from them like the victim of a flash flood. He remembered trembling on the rock ledge, expecting to be hurled into the cascade at any minute.

When the noise and reverberations had ended, and the plume of snow had started to settle, he'd been terrified to board down that lumpy, flash-frozen river in search of Jake, knowing it could flow again at any second and swallow them all. Yet he had been the first to reach for his gear, and he'd been right behind Fiona when she'd identified the site where his childhood friend was buried. Although he and Jake had experienced an off-and-on friendship ever since Peter had moved from Chilliwack, British Columbia, to Seattle — three hours south — their sense of loyalty to each other in times of crisis was never in doubt.

Peter had always admired how decisive Jake was in the heat of the moment and how he (unlike Peter) had a keen sense of other people's feelings. Jake was forever worrying, it was true, but he usually turned the worrying into good decisions, so who cared? He could be a little bossy, which was really bugging Peter lately, and he wasn't as go-for-it on the slopes, but hey, someone had to be the star, and that's my job, Peter thought with a smirk. Jake was as reliable a friend as a guy could want, and Peter was fiercely loyal to him.

Most important, Jake had gotten him this tryout

for weekend work with Sam's Adventure Tours, which he'd wanted to join ever since he and Jake had rafted and kayaked a wild river in northern British Columbia with the outfitter last summer. What could be cooler than being an outdoor guide? He was strong and he loved outdoor adventures. As for the risk — heck, that was just part of the deal. Danger, risk, whatever. But *reading* about avalanches and taking classes about avalanche safety and rescue were one thing. Watching an avalanche sweep past your feet and steal your best friend was another altogether. This avalanche, coming right after the shock of witnessing a helicopter crash and touching two dead bodies ... Peter swallowed. Too much for one day. Too much for a lifetime.

"Peter," Moses was shouting from the top of a very tall snow chunk nearby. "Stay down there till Jake and Fiona get up here. I've kicked steps for them. You're sweep, okay?"

Sweep. That meant last. So now *Moses* was leader and ordering him around. What was with him and Jake, treating him like a servant? Then he remembered. The tail-end person was supposed to be one of the strongest. Jake had been demoted to center position, where the weakest go — because he looked shaken from being buried alive. Peter smiled and straightened his broad shoulders as he let Jake go by.

Then Fiona, snowboard tucked under one arm, her impossibly long hair swaying behind her, scrambled up the boulder. Strong girl, and the avalanche had obviously helped shake her out of her own shock.

Peter applied a few swift kicks to Moses' toeholds to widen them. No way to treat his new snowboard boots, he grumped to himself, but whatever it took to get back up this mess before another slide buried their gear. Slides don't usually strike twice in the same place, he remembered Nancy teaching them, but "hangfires" — big chunks of snow left near the crown by the first slide — could easily collapse and cause a second, smaller release.

Peter didn't like the way the wind had picked up. He didn't like the angry look of the sky or the cold blasts of windblown snow that blinded him every few minutes. He especially didn't like that Joe, Sam, and Nancy were now thirty minutes late and no one had said a thing about it. He figured everyone was waiting for Moses to say what they didn't want to believe: that Joe had been turned back by this storm. There! He'd said it, at least to himself: the S word. Storm. They were in the teeth of a bad one, and if they didn't get back to their gear and hunker down out of reach of avalanches immediately, they'd have more to worry about than when Joe was returning for them. Worries like frostbite or snow blindness or hypothermia. Stuff from Nancy's classes he'd never really thought he'd have to know about. And he was only halfway through her long-winded lectures.

Tonight was going to be about survival. As if this afternoon hadn't been about that already. He'd have to grill Jake later about how it felt to be inside an avalanche. Scary as hell, no doubt, but what a tale he'd have to tell the rest of his life. He'd probably get interviewed on TV and everything. Peter paused as he caught up to Fiona, who was having trouble negotiating her way the last three stories up to the ledge.

"Kind of like climbing over a field of wrecked cars, eh?" Peter commented.

The red-haired girl barely nodded.

He studied her cool board out of the corner of his eyes. Wondered how it handled. Wondered if she was any good. He'd really been working on his moves lately. Was getting pretty hot, an instructor had told him a few weeks ago. Okay, yeah, that definitely sounded egotistical! But, hey, he *was* getting better. He'd have to check out how good she was.

Although it took only twenty minutes to climb from Jake's burial hole back up to the ledge, Peter wiped what felt like an hour's worth of sweat off his brow. His throat ached for water. He checked his watch as he reached for his water bottle. Only 4:15, yet the dark sky felt like an early nightfall.

"Everyone load up with an equal amount of gear," Moses directed in his quiet way. "And I'd keep that to one gulp," he suggested as Peter lifted his water bottle to his lips.

"Whaa?"

"You've got no idea how long you're going to need to make that bottle last," Moses said.

"But we're surrounded by water, as in snow," Peter pointed out.

"Only if you have a backpack full of fuel bottles that I don't know about to melt it. Eat snow and it lowers your body temperature, remember?"

Turning his back to the avalanche zone, Moses pointed to a boulder in the distance, one barely visible in the driving snow. "We're headed to there."

Peter's face glowered and he was thinking about protesting against moving even farther from the original drop-off point, when Jake spoke in a tired voice. "Out of avalanche zones. Good sighting, Moses."

As everyone turned to their packing, Peter studied Jake. His complexion matched the snow, and he was gathering his gear together as slowly as a sleepwalker, a slight tremor in his hand. That fall had obviously taken it out of him. Fiona, in contrast, was moving like lightning, loading up her daypack with so much stuff that it threatened to burst at the seams. Part of still being in shock, or were they just seeing the real Fiona Kerton in action?

Peter opened his own pack and began jamming in the paraphernalia he'd hauled out of the helicopter less than two hours before. He'd stuffed in only a few items, however, when Fiona squeezed by him and dropped her bulging daypack at Jake's feet. Curious, Peter watched her pick up Jake's huge pack, which Jake had just finished repacking and closing.

If she's looking to test the weight difference between his and hers, she's in for a surprise, Peter thought. Jake's pack had weighed a lot *before* he'd crammed in more. It was a wonder she could lift it, Peter mused. But both his and Jake's jaws moved when, instead of lowering it back to the snow, Fiona slung it up onto her back, clamped her boots into her snowboard, and headed down the slope toward the boulder Moses had identified.

"Attagirl," Peter thought. "Make our Jake feel like a loser just 'cause he might be a little tired from being buried in an avalanche. Make yourself out to be some kind of Amazon heroine." His eyes squinted as he watched her near a horizon line.

"Girl, that's where you stop and look, or better yet, go around," Jake muttered. But Fiona was leaning forward to increase her speed.

"Oh, my god, the helicopter didn't kill her, so she's

going to kill herself," Peter said. "Like we need any more medical emergencies today."

He shook his head as she pulled herself into a tuck, launched herself off the lip of the drop, and, flying through mid-air, reached down, grabbed the tail of her board, then let go and dropped out of sight. A tail grab on a drop she'd never seen before, with an impossibly heavy pack on her back: Who was this idiot?

Jake and Moses, as if on a director's prompt, shouldered their packs, clicked their boots into their skis, and pushed away from the ledge after Fiona. But right away and with no warning, the heavy packs forced them to lean a little too far forward and they both wiped out in the soft snow.

Bummer for them, thought Peter, knowing that his snowboard would glide over the powder more smoothly than their skis would. As Jake and Moses struggled up and carried on, Peter kicked the heel-side edge of his board into the snow and prepared to take off.

Even Jake, with his lighter pack, was swaying like an overloaded mule. Again and again, Jake and Moses tottered and fell. Peter sailed past them but, determined not to fall with his own heavy pack, he couldn't reach Fiona's speed. Meanwhile, Fiona, who had reappeared in their sights upright and unharmed, shrank to a speck in the heavy snowfall as she sped to the rock tower. Peter felt like a fool. He was a *good* boarder, could leave Jake and Moses miles behind most days. But this wasn't real boarding, not with this load.

Wham! To his horror, he plunged face-first deep into the snow with spine-cracking, head-splitting impact. His face stung as his goggles ripped off, and snow ground right up his sleeves and gloves. Hoping to regain his feet before Fiona could see, he reached his arm below him, searching for resistance. Nothing. The soft powder seemed to stretch all the way from China. Finally, he managed enough of a fist-hold to push. That's when his tailbone cried out. Ah, he'd identified the bit of anatomy that had stopped his fall. What a miserable slope, miserable pack, miserable day. Finally, he was up and moving, flanked by Jake and Moses. All three boys opted for a detour around the ledge Fiona had jumped.

She'd better not be smiling when they caught up to her, Peter thought. He couldn't believe he'd been feeling sorry for her, thinking she was in shock. He wasn't sure he liked her one bit. She should've waited for the rest of them, anyway.

As the wind and snow pelted them harder each minute, they kept their eyes on the destination boulder, where Fiona stood waiting. After fifteen minutes of misery, Peter and his companions reached the minimal shelter of the rock, which sat beside a compact drift under a heavy crust. Peter eased his bag off, lifted his water bottle, and directed a dribble of water to his parched lips. Jake shed his pack and crumpled to the ground without bothering to remove his skis.

"Park your skis and pull out your shovels," Moses shouted above the wind. "Start tunneling upward into this drift, but don't work so fast that you sweat. We need to keep our clothing dry and save every drop of energy we have."

"I don't have a shovel," Fiona said.

"Use your board," Peter ordered, then turned to Moses. "We're building a snow cave?" he asked, again feeling the sting of being told what to do. "You don't think our tent will hold up in this stor … this wind?"

Moses nodded without looking up.

Peter pulled his shovel off his pack and worked directly behind Moses, passing snow out of the forming tunnel to Fiona and Jake. Soon they were working like a well-trained fire brigade, changing places every half hour to keep the front person fresh. Not unlike a team breaking trail, Peter reflected. He kept an eye on Jake, whose breaks from the job grew steadily longer and more frequent, though he never once complained and was keeping up a valiant front. Fiona, despite sagging shoulders and an increasingly set jaw, worked steadily.

It took three hours to build the cave. They had to pull their headlamps from their packs halfway through the job. Once they'd carved an upward-sloping entry tunnel and a little crawlspace for collecting the cave's cold air, they began forming a lumpy sleeping platform. Peter was amazed how warm and silent the place was. He quickly shed his parka as he helped sculpt the cave walls. Fiona, between leveling the floor with one edge of her snowboard, pushed heaps of snow to Jake, who worked to keep the tunnel clear.

"It's big enough," Moses observed at length.

"Take a break, Jake," Peter said, "while Fiona hauls the bags in." He watched Moses run his glove along the ceiling to smooth it, then produce a candle and matches from his pack, light the candle, and run its flame slowly across the ceiling. Peter wished he'd known how to build a snow cave, wished he'd been the one to coach everyone for the operation.

"Moses, what the heck are you doing?" he asked.

"Making a smooth ceiling so it doesn't drip on us too much in the night."

"Oh. Brilliant," was all Peter could think to say.

Just then, Fiona, wriggling up the tunnel on her stomach, untied the last pack from her ankle, and shoved it toward Jake, who was sitting cross-legged on a corner of the tent the boys had packed for tonight's camping. It was to have held Sam, Nancy, and the three young guides.

Fiona cocked her head and pounced to pull the tent out from under him. "This will make a super floor," she said. "I'll help you unroll it. Then we can unpack everything without stuff getting so wet."

Peter and Jake looked at each another. *Pushy girl*, Peter thought. A granola bar dropped from a pack tipped over by Fiona's tent-yanking. Jake's left hand shot out and clutched it; his right hand unwrapped it and jammed it into his mouth. Peter's mouth watered just watching Jake's cheeks in motion, but he'd have fought anyone who tried to take it from Jake, who clearly needed a boost.

Twenty minutes of ceiling work later, Moses switched off his headlamp and allowed his usually masked face to break into a smile. "Just in time. It's pitch black and absolute hell out there, and cozy as North Pole headquarters in here."

"So all we need is Rudolph's nose to guide Nancy's sleigh to us," Peter suggested. He caught Fiona eyeing him strangely. He didn't care.

"No vehicle will be flying these skies until this storm blows itself out," Moses said. He planted his candle in a small pile of snow. Two clicks sounded as Jake and Pete turned off their lights to save batteries. "Not even my dad would tackle this. It could be a day or two, or even more. Lucky for us we were able to grab some food from Fiona's helicopter."

Although everyone had known for an hour that the storm might have turned Moses' dad back, sober silence hung in the air. Peter had a strange urge to crawl into his sleeping bag and collapse. Fiona declared, "Since it's from my helicopter, I'll take charge of rationing it." She began to search the gear bags and sort all foodstuff into one backpack. Moses shrugged, Jake stared, and Peter shot Jake another "bossy broad" look. Who'd invited her? Hadn't they just saved her life?

Soon, the four cave residents were staking a spot to lay their camping pads and sleeping bag — or, in Fiona's case, her parka — atop the laid-out tent.

"I get nearest the door," Fiona declared as Peter dropped his bag there.

"Says who?" he demanded. He'd never felt so tired. All he wanted to do was sleep.

"I must have it. That's all," she replied in a voice so vehement that Peter couldn't be bothered to argue further. He moved to the spot between Moses and Jake.

Amazing to Peter, the temperature of the cave was so comfortable from one lit candle and their body heat that no one felt obliged to crawl into sleeping bags right away. Instead, Jake and Peter stretched their stiff bodies out slowly, head to toe, as Moses fiddled with his one-pot stove, and Fiona took lessons on how to light it. Peter sniffed the air with anticipation as Fiona and Moses poured four cups of weak tea and placed four steaming bowls of oatmeal into their eager hands a short while later. Huddled cross-legged in their cramped quarters, candlelight flickering on the cold, sculpted walls, they sat on their sleeping bags and gulped down the food and drinks. Peter savored the warmth in his stomach but dreaded how thoughts of what had happened that day were crowding in now that the group had no more chores to distract them. Moses' and Jake's faces looked grim. Fiona had buried her face in her arms. He guessed everyone was thinking about the helicopter crash, the two deaths, and the avalanche. Clearly, no one wanted to talk about it.

"We need to do a gear inventory," Moses said at length. Peter felt relieved someone had found another distraction. "What have we got?"

"We have sleeping bags. Fiona doesn't," observed Jake.

Fiona lifted her head. "I was just doing a day trip. I have only spare gloves, an extra sweater, two water containers, and a chocolate bar."

"Peter, what did you salvage from Fiona's helicopter?"

"Not much — only what I could lash onto or stuff

into our backpacks: an ax, a blanket, a bunch of energy bars, two water bottles, a sandwich, and the pilot's sleeping bag and pad, which were stashed behind his seat, I s'pose for emergencies. They're in Jake's and my backpacks. We already had oatmeal, sandwiches, some freeze-dried soup and supper packets, and a first-aid kit in ours. Fiona can have the pilot's sleeping bag."

"Thank you," came a muffled voice.

"I would have taken clothing off the pilot's body, but I couldn't handle it," Peter admitted.

He regretted saying it the minute he saw Fiona's chest do the heaving thing again, and her face go back into a battle against emotion. She had to be worrying about her parents worrying. She was supposed to be down the mountain and celebrating with them by now. Not stuck here with three strange guys. At least Sam, Joe, and Nancy knew they had camping gear.

He saw Jake shiver despite the extra sweater he'd just pulled on. All four of them went quiet, as if hoping the screeching wind outside, barely audible in their soundproof chamber, might pry away thoughts of what they'd left behind.

"Why did you bring us so far down the slope?" Peter asked Moses.

"You should know that from Nancy's first wilderness-survival course," Moses replied. "We needed to get totally clear of avalanche danger, and I guessed this might be a sturdy drift 'cause it's on a lee side of a boulder, on a bench. It's made a great shelter."

"Can your helicopter find us here when the weather clears?" Fiona ventured.

"No question," Moses said with confidence. "Especially with your helicopter missing, both Sam's Adventure Tours and Search and Rescue will be swarming the top of this mountain when the storm lifts. All we'll have to do is slide out of our cave and wave."

Peter brightened at this news. "So we sit tight, play lots of cards, tell stories, and diet until blue skies return."

"You got it," Moses said.

"What would we do if this storm lasted several days and then no one showed up?" Jake asked from where he lay sprawled on his sleeping bag. Everyone turned his way. No one replied.

"You know, just as a hypothetical situation? Pretend it's a question on Nancy's test," he offered with a tight smile as he climbed into his sleeping bag, the first to do so. Peter frowned at Jake's flat, slow voice, his pale face, and slow movements. Even in the flickering light, he looked out of it. Peter wanted to answer the question, wanted everyone to look at him as he dispensed the correct answer, but heads turned instead to Moses. Moses rubbed his chin, then looked up. "Well, we'd be pretty much out of water ..."

"But we could melt snow," Fiona suggested.

"... and out of fuel, especially if we melted snow. So we'd be desperate to get to treeline for wood to start a fire. Trouble is, once we were in treeline, we'd be harder to spot from the air — not great for getting rescued — and we'd have wildlife to worry about. And if we kept heading down, we'd run out of snow and have to hike in our ski and snowboard boots. But the nearest towns, Pemberton and Mt. Currie, are only a day or two's hike from here, all going well."

"Good thing we're going to be rescued by helicopter tomorrow morning bright and early instead of all that," Peter piped up. "Bacon, eggs, and sticky cinnamon buns at Hicksville Diner."

Moses responded with a thumbs-up, then raised a finger to his lips and jerked his head toward Jake, who was fast asleep. Everyone understood. Stripping to their thermals, climbing into their sleeping bags, fluffing jackets and sweaters into makeshift pillows, they murmured good night to one another. Moses blew out the candle.

Peter imagined the outside wind singing a lullaby to all four occupants of this snug clamshell. He fell asleep so quickly and deeply that no one and nothing could have roused him well into the next day.

5   Sleepover

When Jake awoke their first morning in the snow cave, he wasn't immediately sure where he was. But as he cast sleepy eyes about the dim dome littered with huddled bodies, it all came back. The accident, the rescue, the avalanche, and the exhausting task of building their temporary shelter. Even with a full night's sleep, he felt totally spent. Stiff, sore, and like he could sleep another million years. Not a body was stirring yet. Although his watch said it was nearly noon, little light penetrated the thick snow walls or crept up the tunnel to their small platform.

He took his time wriggling out of his bag and stepping over Fiona. He felt so weak, he couldn't have hurried if he'd tried. He slid down the tunnel, got to his feet, and braced into blinding gusts of wind to pee. Yikes! The gale seemed capable of turning him into a kite, and frozen private parts before breakfast was not his idea of a morning wake-up call.

He returned to find Peter and Moses rolling over to fasten their eyes on Fiona's hot cocoa–making efforts. She served the drinks with portions of crumbled sandwiches that each of the boys had brought for yesterday's lunch. He wondered if she, like him, was just going through the motions, hiding a shattered body and mind. Feeling like something catastrophic was going to happen again any second, no matter how illogical that was. Plagued by the sense that walking ten steps was going to drain every ounce of strength.

"Hey, we can't survive on this," Peter protested. "Jake, Moses, and I packed plenty — enough to eat heartily during a two-day storm — and I'm the one who grabbed stuff from your helicopter. You can live off what little you brought for your day trip and beg some food off us."

Jake watched Fiona lean an elbow on the food sack, narrow her eyes, and stare Peter down, as if daring him to say more or move toward her. Moses' quiet voice broke the standoff.

"We don't know how long before this windstorm will break. Rationing makes sense, and having one person in charge of rationing also makes sense. Better Fiona than you, Peter. You're not known far and wide for long-term planning."

Jake observed Peter dig his fingers into the base of

the cave wall to form a snowball. "Moses is right," Jake said wanly, unable to face an argument of any kind. "We can stuff ourselves with what's left when Nancy picks us up. Until then, I wonder if it's safe to keep food here in the shelter with us. Aren't there wolves and other wild animals up here? Didn't natives used to bury food under piled stones as caches when they traveled in winter?"

He stopped and his eyes darted to Moses. Had he accidentally put his companion on the spot?

"What did Indians eat?" Fiona asked. Jake winced at the word "Indians," then realized an English girl wasn't likely to know the correct terms in Canada were Aboriginal, native, or First Nations. Not that he was about to tell her.

"How would I know?" Moses said, voice calm but eyes growing dark as he surveyed each and every one of them in turn. "I do know there aren't wolves and such above snowline." The tone was even, neither friendly nor angry, Jake judged. The cave was quiet, like a hushed class waiting for a guest storyteller to begin. Jake caught a flicker of animation in his friend's face and watched him open his arms to rest them on his lap.

"You want to know why I don't know about First Nations' old ways." He sounded slightly annoyed, slightly amused. He was studying them, deciding.

"When my dad was little, he got marched away from my grandfather's home by people who wanted to stamp out all our ways. Lots of children were, back then. My grandfather was one of the few of his generation who wasn't put in a residential school — a dormitory away from home. So my grandfather could answer your question, but he only taught me a little before he died. Granddad was afraid to teach my father traditional ways or his language, Yinka Déné, when Dad was young and came home on visits, because that stuff was outlawed. So my father never got to know his father and couldn't teach me. Enough already?"

"No, please go on," Fiona urged.

Jake, too, was hoping Moses would be okay to keep on. Moses had never told them these things before, and Jake couldn't remember learning it in school. Moses reached for a water bottle and poured some water in the little cooking pot. He took his time lighting the stove.

"Dad was forced into a residential school a hundred miles from home and not allowed to speak anything but English, eat what he was used to eating, or act in any way normal — normal to him. He was beaten a few times to make sure he understood that. He wasn't allowed to even mention his little brother, who froze to death trying to escape and hike home in the middle of winter."

The water had boiled. He poured himself a cup, plopped in a teabag, took a sip, and set it down. He crossed his arms and began studying a far wall of the snow cave. His features turned hard and impenetrable. Jake uncrossed his own legs and began organizing the backpacks. He respected the sign that story time was over. He appreciated that Moses had shared it with them, without the anger he probably had every right to feel. He felt they'd been presented with a small gift, food for thought. He felt, well, *moved*.

The steady drip, drip of water from a fault in the ceiling to a cup someone had placed on the floor to collect it was their only distraction over the next five minutes. Jake wondered who was going to break the silence, and if they'd do so before he drifted off.

"Well, there's no going outside today," Peter finally observed. "I've got a little magnetic checkerboard set if anyone wants to launch a checker tournament. From now till dark."

Jake closed his eyes and curled up in his sleeping bag. "Go for it, but count me out on this round."

"Draughts?" Fiona asked shyly as she watched Peter produce the board. "You call draughts 'checkers,' don't you? I'll give it a go."

For two hours, till they could stand it no more, the three played checkers as Jake drifted into and out of sleep. He joined them when they ate a quarter of an energy bar each for lunch and allowed themselves sips of water every few hours. He overheard them worrying aloud about the snow cave roof starting to sag from the moisture inside. They ended up deciding it wouldn't collapse. They worried aloud about what Joe, Nancy, and Sam must be thinking. For the first time, Moses and Peter recounted yesterday's events, telling Fiona what they'd witnessed. She listened quietly, twisting her hands in her lap, holding her chin up. She offered nothing about her experience, and no one pressed. Jake understood her inability to talk. As he half-slept some more, they played cards with Peter's card deck, read paperback books they had brought, and each had a try at a book of crossword puzzles Fiona still had in her pack from her flight from London.

When Jake finally sat up, they challenged one another to sit-up contests (Fiona won), then a push-up marathon (Peter won), and finally a one-armed push-up competition (Jake won, even though it took everything out of him). They dragged some snow in for a snow-sculpting festival, and voted Moses' figure of a bear the best.

"Where did you learn to snowboard?" Jake asked Fiona, curious. "There aren't mountains in England, are there?"

"I learned on special constructions covered in

rubber mats — sort of like artificial turf that gets you sliding, but burns you when you fall down. I've also boarded in ski resorts in France and Switzerland. I used to race in Europe, but I'm not into racing any more."

"Could've fooled me," Peter said. Jake watched Fiona's eyebrows raise, then watched her straighten her shoulders and turn away with her crossword book. Peter's overly cheerful tone hadn't masked the sarcasm, Jake decided. Fiona didn't join into their banter again for a long time.

Hours later, they flopped down on their sleeping bags.

"I am so bored," Peter whined. "If I wasn't afraid of being blown off the mountain, I'd go jog around the outside of the cave. Now I know what cabin fever is. And what an empty stomach feels like."

But he doesn't know what it feels like to have been buried in an avalanche, Jake thought. How it feels even a day later, like I'm still there. Crushed. Numb. Like everything is gray and flat, and I have no feelings any more. Aloud, he said, "It's almost suppertime. I'll fix us some soup."

"How long can storms last here?" Fiona asked.

"Two or three days at most, usually," Moses replied. "This is Day Two. It has only been twenty-four hours, you know."

"More like twenty-four days," Peter grumped. "And it doesn't smell too good in here either. Where's the shower facility?"

"Snow baths are available for free," Moses suggested, digging his hand into a wall to make a snowball. Soon, Moses and Peter lit into a snowball fight. An hour later, Jake sipped his soup, wondering how much longer they'd be trapped in their cave, and what the next day would bring.

The others seemed so certain of rescue. They were counting on being home tomorrow. For some reason, he could not. And this fear, illogical as he knew it to be, gnawed at him hour after hour. It was the reason he suggested a no-headlamps policy that evening. So they told ghost stories around a candle until the pounding wind lulled them to sleep once again.

6   Midnight Chat

J ake woke in the middle of the night to a scrabbling sound. Willing it to go away so he could go back to sleep, he tried crawling deeper into his bag. But his ears were on high alert. He could see nothing in the dark, and his nose could identify nothing but the smell of sweaty bodies. Outside, the wind must be pounding the walls of the cave like giant jackhammers, but he could hear only an echo through its thick walls. Their tent would surely have been shredded by now, and even in their winter sleeping bags, they'd have been half hypothermic without the insulation of these snow walls. The cave, though small, felt comfortable and safe. Or did it?

"Crunch, crunch," came the sound again, this time from the entryway. Someone or something was crawling up the tunnel. He sat bolt upright and reached for his headlamp, teeth clenched. What creature would be out in a storm like this and above treeline? Moses had promised them no animals came above treeline. As he shone the light toward the dark tube, he noticed that Fiona's sleeping bag was empty. Ah, just a middle of the night need to …

As his headlamp caught her face coming up the tunnel, however, he could tell something was wrong. She was racked with shivering, and her enlarged eyes reminded him of the look she'd had as he helped lift her out of the helicopter.

"Hello?" she whispered, and Jake realized she couldn't tell who was holding the light in her eyes.

He trained the light on his face for a second. "Just me. Are you okay?" He spoke as quietly as possible to avoid waking the others.

"Yeah," she said. But her eyes kept darting back down the tunnel as if ready to dive out again. Jake lifted his light to the domed ceiling to diffuse it and glanced around. Peter and Moses remained fast asleep. He looked at Fiona again. She had seated herself at the edge of the sleeping platform, her chin resting on her arms, which clutched her knees tightly. Her eyes were unnaturally large, her breathing fast. She was rocking back and forth and shaking so much that he knew he had to convince her to crawl back into her sleeping bag. Or should he just switch off the light and leave her to herself? No point embarrassing her by staring. But the second he clicked off the light, he heard her crawl down the tunnel again. Whatever was going on, the girl was in distress, and she was going to freeze out there. He pulled on his sweater and coat, grabbed her sleeping bag and wriggled down after her. She sat huddled in the entryway, half her body wind-whipped in the stormy darkness. Jake curled into the entryway's crawlspace, the one they'd designed to collect the cold air. Even there, the cold all but took his breath away. He clicked his headlamp on, wrapped Fiona's sleeping bag around her, and said, as gently as he could, "What's wrong?"

Although she didn't reply, she edged back from the storm raging outside the tunnel and seemed to appreciate the bag, which she slipped off her shoulders, crawled into, and pulled up to her neck. Neither Jake nor Fiona moved or spoke for a few minutes. At least her breathing, illuminated by puffs of vapor in the cold, came evenly again, and the shivering died down. Jake was beginning to wish he had brought his own sleeping bag when she spoke.

"The worst part was rolling down the hill. The door came open and the guide — seemed like he was trying to jump. Maybe he just fell."

Jake switched off the headlamp to give Fiona privacy when he saw a tear roll down her cheek.

"Ever been at a carnival and ridden one of those

glass bubbles that spin as the ride goes 'round?" she asked. But she didn't wait for a reply. "You *know* it's going to stop sometime. You know your door's going to open. And that someone will be there to help you out." She paused. "Wish I'd blacked out till you found me. I'd have been better off. I'm claustrophobic, Jake. I have a fear of enclosed spaces, especially in the dark. That's why I can't be in the snow cave right now. It's why I sleep near the tunnel door. I come out when it gets too bad."

Jake, feeling very awkward, rested one hand on her shoulder. He remembered Peter telling him how she'd grabbed his ankle and wrist. Peter had said she was gasping and had bug eyes. Jake remembered how she'd recovered quickly once out of the helicopter. He tried to imagine being claustrophobic and trapped in that bubble for half an hour with a dead pilot.

"You've really been through it," he said, removing his hand. "But claustrophobia — lots of people have that." *He* didn't, and he didn't know anyone who did, but it felt like the right thing to say. Then he remembered having to help Peter up and down a wall in a cave last year. Fear of heights. What was that called?

"Peter has acrophobia," he bumbled on. "He can't handle looking down from tall places. So you see? It's no big deal. We all have our little things. I won't tell the others if that's what's bothering you."

"Thank you," she said. "So what's your little thing? If we all have little things, like you say."

Jake thought for a minute. "I worry all the time. Peter calls me a grandma."

"It's sensible to worry a bit," Fiona replied, "especially since you're a natural leader. What's your little thing, *really?*"

Jake couldn't think what to say but felt forced to come up with something, anything. "My dad left us a few years ago after a big fight with my mom. He never said goodbye, never wrote, has never phoned or anything. Maybe that's why I worry so much. I worry about money, and my mom, and where my dad is and why. Some day I'm going searching for him."

Dark as it was, Jake could feel Fiona turn and study him. "You'll find him one day, Jake. I know it. And he'll be proud of how you've turned out. I want my dad to be proud of me some day, but I don't dare tell him my plans. Know what I'm going to do after school?"

"Be a doctor, you said, like your dad."

"A doctor, but not like my dad. I'm going to join Médecins Sans Frontières. That's French for 'Doctors Without Borders.' They help poor countries or places with wars going on."

"Cool," Jake said. "Why wouldn't your dad go for that?"

"He's a worrier, like you." She wriggled in her bag as if trying to draw more warmth from it. "He must be worried sick about me right now. And if your mom knew how close you came yesterday, she'd be ever so concerned."

British understatement, Jake mused.

The wind howled through the next lull in conversation.

"I can't stop reliving it. I can't stop being scared. I can't concentrate on anything," Jake said.

"I know," said Fiona. "But we pulled you out, and you need to pull yourself out the rest of the way. We need you in case anything else goes wrong."

Why? Jake wondered. He didn't want to be a "natural leader" any more, if he ever was. He just wanted to go home and go to sleep. He just wanted to feel safe again.

"Thank you for bringing me my sleeping bag," Fiona was saying. "It's crazy, isn't it, not being able to sleep in a small space?"

"What if you had my headlamp? Would that make a difference?"

"I could go back up there then, yes. Just knowing I could flick it on …"

Jake placed his headlamp in her hand. "Good night, Fiona. I won't tell anyone about your claustrophobia."

Half-frozen, he swiveled around in the cramped

crawlspace, wriggled up the tunnel, and leaped into his sleeping bag, never so appreciative of a warm bed. Fiona followed him a moment later, and within minutes, her deep breathing signaled to Jake that she'd fallen asleep. Jake himself fell asleep dreaming of clutching a hot water bottle.

7   The Plane

Alll four youths were dead asleep when the drone of a small plane sounded above the next morning. Peter, like his mates, was simply too far gone to roll out of his sleeping bag, slide down the tunnel, and wave before the aircraft was gone.

But it didn't take him long to jump-start himself into packing his bag and vacating the snow cave when he realized a plane was in the area. Outside the entrance, scanning the sky overhead, Peter leaped up and kicked his heels. "Blue sky!" he shouted, high-fiving Jake as Fiona and Moses smiled. Even the gusts of wind that blew snow into their faces seemed friendly. They plopped down on their backpacks to wait. Within minutes, Peter realized that the clear skies had brought with them a big drop in temperature, sharpened by the bite of the wind. He pulled his hat down over his cold ears and scanned the sky again.

"Do you think they'll spot us for sure? Maybe we should spread out, get away from the shadow of this boulder."

"We should stay together," Moses said, "but let's move out of the shadow. I'm just going back in the snow cave to see if I dropped a strap for my backpack." He crouched down and crawled up the tunnel.

Move out of the shadow. Peter took this to mean moving by snowboard. He clicked in and took off, thrilled to be able to move again after two days cramped in a snow shelter. He knew not to go far. He knew to go slowly. He knew to keep his head up, alert for a slide. In fact, his head kept lifting way up, looking for that plane. He felt like leaping and dancing. But he restrained himself, sliding just a little way down the slope to a small hollow.

A minute later, he heard Moses shouting. He turned and looked back. He couldn't hear what Moses was saying, but Jake and Fiona were following him, Jake moving like an out-of-it zombie who'd follow anyone anywhere, and Fiona sticking close to Jake, as if sensing he needed keeping an eye on. As the plane's drone sounded again, Peter searched the sky. He loved feeling the bright sunshine on his face, was pleased they'd moved out of the cold shadow, was excited a plane was searching for them. How he wanted to be rescued! What a story he'd have to tell back home!

As Fiona and Jake neared Peter, Moses began barreling down the gusty slope behind them, shouting and waving like a crazed sasquatch.

"Stop!" he was saying.

"Okay, already," Peter shouted back, annoyed at Moses' bossiness, as Jake and Fiona stopped beside him. Peter studied Jake's expressionless face and the dark circles beneath his eyes. Not looking any more alert today. Peter figured he'd better take charge. Yes, good idea. He could handle that.

He, Jake, and Fiona were shading their eyes looking up into the brilliant sky for the plane, which they could hear but not see, when Moses, face puffed with anger, pulled up to join them. No doubt he was going to say Peter had gone a little further than he'd meant him to. No doubt he was going to deliver a preachy lecture on not staying together, Peter thought.

But he never got a chance, because just then, the snow beneath him collapsed like a rotten trap door. One loud crack and Peter felt his legs give out from under him. He was free-falling. *Bam.* A cold ice floor bruised him. As he lay in a stunned heap, he felt snowflakes sting his face, as if the last pieces of the snow bridge over the hidden crevasse wanted to camouflage him. He groaned and tried to roll over, striking his head on the wickedly hard, cold ice wall beside him. Panic seized him, made him grab for something to help him up. His flailing arm touched nothing but snow, ice, and shadows. He looked up, only to see crevasse walls tower to twenty-five feet above. He looked left and right, counted four bodies strewn in the crevasse's bottom, cushioned only by the remains of the crevasse's former snow covering.

Peter had landed on his back — or rather, on the backpack attached to his back. He struggled up until his head was resting against one ice wall, boots still firmly attached to the snowboard, which was pitched against the other ice wall like a crooked shelf. Two and a half stories above, the blue sky peered at them like light from a narrow skylight. Peter watched a passing plane — *their* rescue plane — disturb the perfect stripe of blue for a split second. No way the plane's occupants could see into this pit, which was no more than five feet wide where he sat, he thought with horror.

He dared not move more as he tried to assess whether he was injured. Taking deep breaths to steady his nerves, he became aware of someone's head pressing into one leg and turned to identify Jake, curled into a ball except for skis splayed in opposite directions. Jake was blinking at the crevasse wall against which Peter's snowboard rested.

"Jake, you okay?" Peter asked, still hesitant to move himself.

"My side. Bruised bad."

Slowly, Peter unwound himself and, with two clicks, removed his board. He leaned over Jake, saw that his face resembled a gray mask. He turned as Fiona scrambled over.

"I'll check him over. See to Moses," she suggested.

"Moses?" Peter asked, crawling over to the fourth figure in their fissure.

"I'm good. Got more padding than you guys to fall on," Moses responded. "Got the breath knocked out of me, that's all. I'll move in a second. Peter, why the …"

"I know. I went too far." What could he say? The gravity of the situation was pressing in on him worse than the cold of their icebox. He expected Moses to yell at him, knew he deserved the wrath of everyone down here. So he was floored at Moses' next words.

"My fault, too. I didn't see it. I was too mad at you to be paying close attention. And they're murderously hard to spot, but I might have seen it if I'd looked more carefully."

"What are?" Peter asked.

"Crevasses under a new snowpack. Nothing to warn a person but maybe a tiny dent in the snow."

Peter's mind flashed back to the hollow. He, Jake, and Fiona had all been standing in it safely enough. It had taken Moses to break the snow bridge's back. But this wasn't Moses' fault, Peter knew. He, Peter, had moved too far from the boulder. It was the excitement of hearing the plane. *The plane.* He hung his head. They had to get out of here fast.

"You're too impulsive and excitable," Peter's dad was always saying. "You need to focus and take more responsibility." Peter felt his shoulders sink.

"Bruised," Fiona ruled as she finished examining Jake. "Bruised, not broken. Bruised ribs, one bruised ankle. Pretty lucky, considering."

Peter peered at Jake, at his limp body and vacant eyes. Lucky? Like Jake had needed any more falls. He turned and studied Moses, saw him look up the crevasse. Peter knew Moses wanted to say something encouraging about being able to climb out, but couldn't.

"All we need is crampons, rope, and an ice ax," Peter muttered.

"Crampons are those pointy metal things that attach to bottoms of boots, right?" Fiona asked. "For climbing up ice. Do we have any?"

"No, but we have rope and an ax," Peter replied in as positive a tone as he could muster.

Crack! Peter turned to see Jake breaking an icicle off the wall beside him to shove down his socks. "To keep the swelling down," he explained. "A flare would be even better to get us rescued. Peter, are you sure you didn't find a flare in the helicopter and stick it in your pack?"

"No." Peter hung his head again. Had there been one and he'd missed it? He'd pulled so many things out so fast. But he'd wanted to get out of there, like everyone else. He hadn't seen a flare.

"They're up there looking for us. They'll look for at least two days," Moses said. His face was long and ashen. His shoulders slumped.

"Will they send a ground party we can shout up to?" asked Fiona.

Moses studied the floor of their crevasse as if searching there for an answer. "Maybe," he said in a low voice, then lifted troubled eyes. "The avalanche danger is extreme after that storm. And we're nowhere near where they dropped us off. They'll figure out what happened with Fiona's helicopter. They'll know we probably tried to help, probably got pulled down with it in the avalanche. They may not land a ground party, especially if they see no sign of us above."

"The snow cave! They'll see that! Or our tracks from the snow cave to here!" Fiona insisted.

Moses turned away. "The wind was covering our tracks faster than we could make them, and they'd never identify a snow cave from the air. Our only hope is to climb out of here." He peered up, face desolate.

Peter jumped up and walked seventy-five giant paces to where the ice walls curved, met, and lifted straight up like the front hull of a ship. He ran his glove along the seam and stared up to where the out-of-reach prow joined the mountain's surface. He turned around and marched back to the huddled group, stepped over them, and shuffled twenty-five steps to the rear hull of their ice boat — this one a vertical wall of snow nearly as hard as ice. He punched his fist into it as hard as he could, then nursed the bruise it caused. He kicked the snow wall with his boots, then pounded it like a child wanting out of his room. Eventually he sank down to his knees. Moses rose and walked over to place his hands on Peter's shoulders.

"We'll think of something," he said. "We'll find a way out. We have six hours of daylight left to find a way. Meantime, we need to stay warm. It's way, way colder here than up top."

"Why is that?" asked Fiona, pulling her red parka closer around her.

"Because we're surrounded by ice, not snow. Snow is a good insulator. That's why our snow cave was pretty warm. Sleeping down here tonight will suck. It's midday now and there's not a sliver of sunshine."

Peter yanked the rope from his pack, unwound it, and looped it like a lasso. He held the loop in one hand, and the end in the other, and scanned the sides of the crevasse for any form that jutted out and might catch the rope and hold them. There was nothing. Nothing at all. Just smooth, vertical, glassy walls. Peter was amazed by the utter silence down here, save for the drip, drip of water. Like a sound-proof chamber.

He turned and threw one end of the rope up. It fell back on top of him. He tied various items from his pack to that end, and threw like a baseball pitcher encouraging a pop fly. After a dozen fruitless attempts to secure a hold, he sank to the cold floor and placed his head in his hands. He felt Jake rest a hand on his shoulder, but Jake said nothing. For once, Jake wasn't telling Peter what to do, but for once, Peter wanted him to. What was with Jake? How could they snap him out of his funk?

Eventually, Peter rose again. He grabbed the cold handle of the ax and walked the full perimeter of their dungeon, looking for a wall that offered something other than a vertical wall or an overhang. Although defeated in this search, he started in on a vertical wall anyway, pounding with the ax till he had sculpted one foothold. As Peter stood in this foothold, braced by Moses from behind, he cut another. But even with Fiona and Moses using Fiona's snowboard to prop him up there as he cut a third foothold, he knew there was no going further. They'd just fall to the ground — with an ax that could land on top of them.

"If only it were a true ice ax," Peter despaired. "The

teeth of ice axes hold so well that a climber with one in each hand can climb a frozen waterfall like Spiderman."

The exertions had warmed him but had also made him hungry and thirsty.

"Fiona, what's for lunch? Not that we had breakfast," Peter asked, biting his lip as he scanned Jake's zombie-like face again.

She rummaged through the food pack. "Soup, oatmeal, powdered eggs, or dried beef stroganoff, if there's enough fuel and water. After that, we're down to a few energy bars."

Fear registered itself on every face even before Moses spoke: "We're critically short of water now. Two days, max. And even worse for fuel. But I'll make eggs. We need energy to get out of here or it won't matter what we've got for grub." He pulled out his stove and measured water into the pan with all the care of a pioneer banker weighing gold.

Meanwhile, all four dug into their packs for extra clothing. Peter noticed that Jake was shivering even after putting on everything he had. Peter dug out Jake's sleeping bag and handed it to him. "Jake," he whispered, "what should we do?"

Jake shrugged his shoulders, struggled into his bag, closed his eyes, and turned away. Fear sliced through Peter. Where was the Jake he knew, the one who could be counted on to tell you what to do whether you wanted him to or not?

"Jake," he appealed again, gently shaking his buddy's shoulders.

"You decide," Jake mumbled without moving.

Peter lifted his head to Moses. The two locked eyes for several seconds. Moses knew stuff, Peter thought — about snow and mountains and crevasses and survival. Why wasn't he offering ideas? He should be helping Peter coax Jake out of his weirdness. But Moses looked away as he said, "You heard Jake. You decide."

Reluctantly, Peter turned to Fiona. She may not have wanted to be part of this disaster, but she was, so why wasn't her bossy nature and intelligence combining to produce some suggestions?

"So, Fiona, got any bright ideas?" he said as casually as he could.

She pursed her lips, pulled out her crossword book, and buried her gaze in it. What was that all about? he wondered. She'd rather freeze to death than work with him on a solution? Or like Jake, she'd already given up?

The shafts of sunlight that had visited the upper reaches of the crevasse shortly after they'd landed here had long since disappeared. Even when Moses served up minute portions of powdered scrambled eggs — the tastiest meal Peter had ever had — he noticed that spirits failed to lift.

"My mother always says that when things look really bad, you have to think of three things to be thankful for," Peter ventured.

"*Thankful for?*" Moses demanded.

"No one was seriously injured during the fall," Fiona volunteered.

"No animals can attack us down here," suggested Jake.

"And I'll lose weight," Moses said, patting his waist, then reddening a little.

"I know the solution," Peter spoke up.

"To not losing weight?" Fiona asked.

"To getting out of here." Everyone turned to Peter. "I climb on Moses' shoulders, Jake climbs on mine, and Fiona on his with the rope looped around her waist. She climbs out and finds a way to pull us out one by one, or to catch the attention of the plane."

"I'm going to hold up three people?" Moses protested.

"Better that than someone trying to hold *you* up," said Fiona. Peter watched her face turn pink. "Sorry," she mumbled.

Peter knew Moses was far more sensitive about his weight than he ever let on.

It took a while to organize themselves for the

strange gymnastics exercise, and Peter worried about Jake's bruised ankle, but soon the operation was underway. Peter stepped into Moses' cupped hands as Moses crouched like a weightlifter. Soon Peter stood wobbling on Moses' shoulders as Jake, guarding his bruised ribs, attempted to climb atop Peter. Only once in numerous tries did Jake manage to get where he was supposed to be, and never did Fiona get to the top of the ever-toppling heap. Peter reckoned that under normal circumstances, they might have had a good laugh about it. But Moses' stoic face, the hunger and tiredness in them all, and the knowledge of what was riding on their success or failure, killed any sense of humor. Long before darkness began to fall, Peter cooked up other schemes: a pyramid formation of bodies, an attempt to chip ice blocks out of the walls to climb onto, an effort to pile backpacks and snow from the floor to climb up. Each failure seemed to bring a new wave of depression and exhaustion. Even the occasional sound of a plane or helicopter above failed to stir the group's hopes or lift their faces after a while, Peter noted with alarm. How could he get them out of this?

Finally, Moses declared aloud what Peter knew everyone was thinking: "We need to prepare ourselves for the night. Frostbite and hypothermia are our biggest enemies."

8   Window and Stairs

D ay Two in the bottom of the crevasse began like the previous morning. The sounds of aircraft overhead shattered Jake's restless sleep.

"A flare, a flare. My kingdom for a flare," Peter, lying beside him, misquoted Shakespeare. No one smiled, replied, or moved.

Jake tried to wriggle his toes. He pictured them blue on the ends of frosted limbs. He touched his stomach. Hunger pains like he'd never known rippled from gut to brain. He ran his tongue across the roof of his mouth trying to remove what felt like cotton balls there.

Pain shot through his ribs as he reached for his water bottle. He'd stowed it against his chest inside his coat, which he was wearing inside his sleeping bag, to keep it from freezing solid. He lifted and shook the bottle, which rattled like a glass of iced lemonade at a summer party. Before he managed to bring it to his dry lips, it slipped from his glove and dropped on the body closest to him. Peter opened his eyes and lifted his head.

"Jake? You okay?"

"Oh, yeah, comfy as a movie star on a private beach," Jake declared. He didn't care about the hurt look that crossed Peter's face, or that Peter turned his head away. What did Peter expect him to say? They were four bodies huddled as tightly together as shivering newborn pups. Everyone was wearing every item of clothing they'd brought inside their sleeping bags, over which they were attempting to share the pilot's blanket, and under which the skewed tent spread like a groundsheet, protected them (but not much) from the bare ice floor.

Jake reached half-frozen gloved fingers toward the edge of the blanket where it had strayed away from him. He watched bursts of shivering move the sea of sleeping bags like life jackets vibrating in the bottom of a motorboat.

The chilling cold of this ice trap was too much to bear. The night had taken a severe toll. The prospect of another day down here — Jake dared not think about another night — was impossibly depressing. Back in the snow cave, there had been contests, snow-ball fights, storytelling, and reading. Even the arguments about who would prepare how much food when had made their time there seem like a resort stay compared with this. Here, there was no energy, no talking, no eating, and precious little drinking. Just bitter cold and sadness and the tension of waiting for a land-rescue party that may or may not appear. Jake was too cold to sleep, too tired to want anything *but* sleep. Which would they die of first, starvation or cold? All the survival stories he had ever read marched through his chilled brain, including stories of adventurers who turned into cannibals as fellow team members expired. His stomach was too empty to turn over at the thought.

As the day wore on, Jake did what he seemed to do best: drift into and out of sleep, sometimes aroused by the drone of a plane. At one point, he forced himself to sit up and reach for the little stove.

"One bowl of oatmeal to share among us," Peter advised, in a gentle but stern tone, like he was Jake's mom or something. Then he leaped up to help Jake prepare the meal. Jake was a little startled by Peter's sudden surge of energy. As far as Jake's foggy brain could recall, Peter had been lying still and morose all morning, staring at the crevasse walls. Worrying. Peter wasn't normally a worrier; that was usually Jake's job.

When Jake, with Peter helping and hovering,

served up the food, neither Moses nor Fiona climbed out of their bags; they just extracted their arms to accept it. Half an hour later, both drifted back to sleep.

Jake, grateful for the food in his stomach and feeling slightly revived, turned to Peter. Peter just kept staring at him.

"Stop looking at me like that," Jake finally said. "Haven't you got any better scenery to stare at?"

"No, strangely enough, it's you or walls of ice, though I'm not sure there's a heck of a lot of difference lately."

"Yeah? Well, who led us all to the crevasse? We'd be sitting pretty in Mt. Currie if you hadn't. And where are you going to lead us next, oh great leader?" Jake really didn't feel like fighting, normally hated sarcasm, but he felt like someone else had taken over his body the last three days.

"You're right," Peter replied, eyes unflinching. "I messed up big-time. It won't happen again, if I ever get a chance to get out of here and prove that."

Jake pulled his wool cap farther down his face and tucked his gloved hands under his armpits. "Well, I award you one point for honesty." He turned his head up to the blue strip of sky and sighed. "And I must have been totally out of it to follow you. But how's this for a challenge: You got us in here. You get us out." And with that, spent both physically and emotionally, Jake crawled back into his sleeping bag, rolled over, and squeezed his eyes shut. Not because he needed to sleep but because he'd never cried in front of Peter before and he wasn't going to start a new tradition now.

He must have drifted off in the end. Hours later — he didn't know or care how many — Jake woke again to feel Peter wriggling out of his sleeping bag. It was afternoon now, judging from the navy blue of what he had come to think of as their attic window. Jake watched Peter crawl to his backpack and unstrap both a shovel and the ax. As he moved away, Moses promptly grabbed Peter's empty sleeping bag and pulled it across Jake, Fiona, and himself.

"Bang, crunch," came an ear-splitting noise behind them.

"What's he doing, digging a tunnel to China?" Jake asked.

"If it's warmer there, that's okay with me," Fiona replied.

"Guys!" Peter shouted at them. "Get out here and help. We're not sleeping this way another night. It's too cold. We're going to make a snow cave in this snow wall."

"Yeah, right," Moses said, sinking deeper into his bag.

"Moses! Jake! Come help!" Peter ordered in a voice

that stirred something inside Jake. He lifted his sore torso to a sitting position and began to slide his bag off his stiff body.

Moses and Fiona just stared at him. Peter pointed his shovel toward them, raised his eyebrows as he registered Jake's movements, and prodded Moses. "Up, up." Moses rose in slow, reluctant motion. Jake grabbed an energy bar, hesitated, then chopped it into four pieces and downed one.

"What about me?" asked Fiona, folding her hand around her share and eyeing the three empty sleeping bags like a thief in waiting.

"You don't have a shovel. Stay where you are," Peter told her.

Jake smiled. Peter may have meant she could stay put, but Jake figured Fiona wasn't likely to take him up on it. Sure enough, by the time the three boys were taking turns pounding on the snow wall with three shovels and the ax, Fiona had joined them, pink snowboard in hand.

"This is nothing like the crusty stuff we made the other snow cave out of," Jake observed, steeling himself for a shovel lunge. He removed his jacket and ran an arm across his forehead.

"It's like ice," Moses agreed.

"We're experienced at this by now," Peter encouraged them. "It's three o'clock and I bet we can finish this snow cave faster than the three hours the other one took. I challenge us to have it ready by five. Another quarter of an energy bar each if we do."

Jake smiled again. Food, competition, and Peter. Peter, competition, and food.

"I'll rattle off my whole repertoire of jokes while we're at it," Peter continued. "Anyone who fails to smile at my jokes gets a shovel full of snow down their parka. What is the difference between a vulture and a lawyer?"

No one answered right away.

"The vulture doesn't get Frequent Flyer points."

"That's not all that clever," Fiona offered.

"Yeah, well, you're so stupid you thought a quarter-back was a refund!" And with that, true to his word and with god-knows-what reserves of energy, Peter launched into more jokes, cajoling, and cheerleading as, indeed, a cave of sorts began to take shape. Jake wanted to collapse into it at the first sign of a hollow, but he smiled at Peter instead. Good old Peter. Always bouncing off walls, always chirpy. Peter was just what a cold crevasse and disheartened crew of teens needed.

When Peter's motor-mouthing finally died down, Fiona surprised them with a short recital of songs — in Latin, of all things.

"I used to be in a choir. We only ever sang in Latin," she admitted. "And I studied Latin in school. It's useful for remembering medical terms."

Now I've heard everything, Jake thought. Finally, as the stripe of sky above their jail began to darken, Peter said, "Ready for move-in."

"I'll second that," Jake said.

They knew the routine. As Fiona dragged the tent in to roll it out as flooring, Jake helped pull bags in. Judging the cave to be too small for both backpacks and full-length bodies, however, he grabbed a shovel to hollow out a storage cubby on the far side of the cave. It took only ten minutes of shoveling and a swift kick of his boots. But as he shoved the first backpack into place, he was astonished to witness the back wall of the closet collapse. He stared. He stared again. There was now a window in his closet, and half the backpack was poking out of it like a cannon from a fortress rampart.

Heart leaping, Jake pulled the bag back in and forced his head through the opening. "Guys, guys, guys!" he shouted. "We're free! We're free!"

Three bodies piled on top of him. Jake crawled out from under them to tumble out onto the floor of the other half of their crevasse, hidden from them until now by the snow wall. He walked ten paces and touched the two-storey-high, inverted snow cone in front of him like a preacher touches an altar.

"An hour of ax work will turn this into stairs," he ruled, voice quivering with excitement.

He glanced up at the evening's first stars, then piled back through the closet window to fetch his headlamp and the shovels. Soon, four sets of arms were applying shovels and ax to sculpt a stairway that rose steadily out of their prison. But as soon as they scrambled onto the mountain's surface, Jake grabbed hold of Peter's arm.

"No more mistakes," he ordered. "We're going to rope together when traveling in crevasse country, we're going to watch for hollows in the snow that mean hidden crevasses, and" — he raised his voice — "*we are not going to travel at night.* We'll sleep in the new snow cave and break camp at first light."

Fiona and Moses nodded. Peter, after a second's hesitation, nodded too. As they filed slowly back down the chinked cone, Peter spoke up. "Energy bar pieces to everyone. And special thanks to Jake for breaking through."

"No, Peter, it was you who broke through," Jake replied, squeezing his buddy's shoulder. "You forced us to keep going when we were giving up."

"It's true," Moses agreed, clapping one hand on Jake's shoulder and one on Peter's.

"Yes," Fiona said, eyes lit with an energy Jake hadn't lately seen in anyone.

Peter shrugged, but not before Jake glimpsed a wide, wide grin.

9   Freedom

Jake awoke in high spirits the next morning. "Treeline," he thought. They could make treeline in maybe five hours, chop wood to make a fire, and melt snow to fill their water bottles and cook up a meal. Or maybe a helicopter or plane would spot and rescue them on their way to the trees. If not, they'd at least be able to have some fun on the slope. Do some real skiing and snowboarding.

He pulled his water bottle out of his sleeping bag and studied it. Exactly one swallow left. Thank goodness they'd found a way out of the crevasse. And last night had been more comfortable with the snow cave's greater insulation.

He rolled over and observed Moses staring at the snow cave's ceiling.

"Treeline today," Jake said, "or rescue on the way there."

Moses continued staring at the dome. Jake, worried, nudged him. "Moses?"

"Uh-huh."

"What're you thinking about?"

"My grandfather."

"What about him?"

Silence again. Jake turned to Moses as Peter and Fiona stirred.

"He once told me never to trap a beaver during spring breakup, but I can't remember why."

Jake sat up and stared at Moses, trying to imagine how the group would cope if Moses went delirious on them. Moses rambled on.

"They used to have dogs good at scenting beavers. They were called *Lheeza*, which means noble dog. It took four beaver skins to make a blanket."

"Moses, why are you talking about beavers?" Jake asked, his chest tightening. "We have to get out of here. There could still be rescue planes today."

"No rescuers," Moses replied, eyes still fixed above him. "We're on our own."

"You don't know that!" Jake insisted, planting his face squarely over Moses' in hopes that a closer look at his friend's eyes would help him determine if Moses was losing it. But Moses closed his eyes and sighed.

"Granddad used to know stuff from dreams. Dad never understood that. But it's Granddad who is with me this trip. He knew the outdoors and survival skills better than Dad or me. Elders are really important in our culture. We're very aware of them, feel sort of guarded by them, even after they die. I keep thinking of things he tried to teach me, stories he wanted me to remember. You wouldn't understand."

Jake, frowning, shoved his damp-sock-padded feet into his cold ski boots. "Okay, Moses. Sorry. I guess I didn't really — don't totally — understand." Fog floated above the crevasse, blotting out what he'd hoped would be a clear blue sky full of rescue aircraft. Never mind. He and his companions were now free of the crevasse and would soon be safely down the mountain one way or another. He stepped out of the cave and crunched over the crevasse floor to the crude steps they'd carved the night before. He ran a glove over one as he replayed yesterday's events. Peter had finally gotten the group moving again. He might not know these mountains like Moses, might not have completed all of Nancy's wilderness survival training, but his high energy, humor, and impulsiveness — stuff Jake sometimes found annoying — had added up to a resourcefulness and never-give-up spirit that had saved them from an ugly fate. Good old Peter. And Peter's energy was just what they needed today to combat Moses' insistence that there would be no rescue planes today.

"Peter, can you lead today?" Jake asked. "We need our best snow rider to blaze us a safe path to treeline."

Peter's head came out of his sleeping bag like a turtle emerging from its shell. His grin looked warm enough to melt the walls of the crevasse. "You got it!" he replied.

Soon they were packed and stampeding up the ice steps, all except Moses, who shuffled. Jake, standing atop the mountain's surface, paused to stare at cannonballs of fog that floated toward them like tumbleweeds in a windstorm. He peered up, only to be hit with the sensation of standing in a low-ceilinged room. Downhill, visibility was better than directly overhead, despite the waves of fog. It was the strangest thing he'd ever seen, but he figured they'd be fine for skiing as long as it didn't sock in any tighter. With luck, he figured, it might even lift enough to let aircraft catch sight of them.

"Guys, we need to rope up for a little while, till we're out of crevasse terrain," Jake decided. "Then Peter can take over to lead us to treeline. And don't forget to turn on your transmitters."

Peter grumbled and Fiona cast a disappointed look Jake's way as she flicked some snow off her board, but Moses offered an approving nod and pulled the rope out of his backpack. As they proceeded downhill, Jake turned to watch Peter, roped near Fiona, deliberately board a little too fast now and again. This forced the rope to tighten between the two of them, pushing her and her board a little off line. She never fell, though.

What was Peter aiming for, a Fiona face plant? Jake wouldn't allow the thread of tension between them to develop. As soon as he'd given everyone permission to detach themselves from the rope, Jake skied over to Peter before Peter had a chance to take up his new leadership mantle.

"Peter," he said out of earshot of the others and leveling a stern gaze at his buddy, "just 'cause she's a good boarder who refuses to be impressed by you doesn't mean you can treat her like that. She's a strong part of this team, has carried her weight from the start. You want to be a leader, you show respect to every member of your team. Be nicer."

Peter cocked his head and smiled. "Say what? Don't know what you're talking about, Jake old buddy. Hey, everyone! I'm leader now. To treeline!"

Jake sighed, but satisfied that he'd made his point, he let his shoulders relax. Though the heavy pack still made him sink farther into the powder than he liked, today's snow cover was easier to negotiate. He listened to the snow's crumpling noise as he rode over it with his heavy load. Like squashing Styrofoam coffee cups, he mused. It felt totally invigorating to run smoothly down the gentle slope, fog or not. He noticed that

Peter was picking the route with a practiced eye, mindful to traverse around piles of rocks and slow down for rough patches of snow. Peter was by far the fastest of the four of them today, but he was still remembering to pause and wait on a regular basis, and to select lines they could all slide with ease, not lines that showed off his perfect carving turns.

Jake smiled and let more tension evaporate from his body as he studied each member of the team in turn. Fiona cut back and forth with no visible effort, jumping now and again to grab her tail, and spinning out 360s with the grace of a skate-dancer. The wispy fog gave her show some special effects. "Makes boarding look easy," Jake thought with respect. He'd never really taken to the sport himself; he liked floating through powder on skis. Pure magic.

Moses had all but grown up on skis, zigzagged through the sometimes waist-deep snow with the precision of a scroll saw, his puffs of breath rising through the mist like cigar rings. Clearly, the skiing had pushed aside his moroseness for now.

Jake himself, though still shaking off the effects of the past few days, felt a tingle of excitement as he tried to follow Moses' moves. He knew he was a strong skier by most standards, even though Peter was fond of telling him he was overcautious and "needed to work on those hot moves." He lifted his fingers to his goggles and wiped them back and forth a few times like windshield wipers. Nothing like shooting the slopes in a cloud, he thought. But it was okay, because he felt like a new person today, as if a curtain had lifted and given him back his life. In some ways, he felt like he'd only just emerged from his burial hole in that avalanche. The freedom from the cave and crevasse and the pure joy of skiing were releasing him at last from a mental fog; so what if a physical fog lingered?

Down the mountain they went, keeping one another in sight despite the waves of vapor that danced about them. Wisps snapped at their ankles, swished downhill ahead of them, and playfully lassoed their bent knees. And yet, like mist in a sauna, the moisture never entirely obscured their view of where they were headed; it just added a gauzy effect accentuated by the thick fog roof that licked their heads.

As the mountain began to drop away faster, Jake followed his teammates with growing exhilaration. He watched as Peter shifted his weight and extended his board to pop off a small lip before pulling a 360-degree tail grab. Had his buddy been at a freestyle snowboard competition, the judges would have awarded his landing an eight out of ten. Jake smiled as he saw Peter glance behind him to ensure that Fiona had seen it all. She went for the same crest at hurricane speed and performed an eye-popping 540 — one and a half turns — on that hot pink board, which seemed to have an invisible fuel tank powering it. Jake wasn't the least surprised when Peter upped the ante over the next hit with a 540 Indie, gloves touching the front edge like a salute to imaginary spectators below.

Okay, guys, tone it down, Jake thought, thankful that as far as he knew, neither Peter nor Fiona could pull off a backflip. He himself skirted the small rises, content to rip through the deep "pow" with no fear of falling on his sore rib cage.

A while later, Jake memorized the way Moses rode a ridge, dodging rocks like an Olympic slalomist, catching air of his own and neatly crossing his skis before succumbing to gravity. Like Peter, Moses pulled off a photo-finish landing. Jake decided to take the same route without the "iron cross." No one behind him to impress, he reasoned.

But half an hour later, after watching Peter, Fiona, and Moses all buy air off a modest cliff over a soft run-out, he decided to go for it. Easing off his edges, he faced straight downhill and raced to the cliff to achieve the speed he wanted, then took to the air on invisible upward rails, savoring the rush of wind past his ears, the kiss of mist against his face. He was one with his skis and pack, enthralled by the perfect quietude.

Then his body and skis began hurtling toward Earth. His sense of oneness took flight as he scanned the snow anxiously. He blinked and flinched, felt the gully rise to meet him.

Whomp! The deep powder embraced him like a blanket. He blew snow out of his mouth and nose, placed a hand on his ribs and admitted that nothing had been hurt but his ego. Maybe the rest hadn't even seen.

Dream on. Three pairs of legs whooshed to the rim of his downy nest. Peter's flicker of concern soon gave way to the infamous Montpetit belly laugh, accompanied in harmony by low chuckles from Moses and lyrical giggling from Fiona. Hmmph. At least Moses was acting normal again, Jake decided. But as Peter pulled him to his feet, he could feel his own face generating a 150-watt smile.

"That was too fun," he declared. "Totally worth it."

"I reckon we're two-thirds the way to treeline now," Moses asserted. He'd hardly finished speaking when they heard a helicopter approach overhead. As everyone lifted their eyes, Jake felt his heart push against his chest. He cursed the thick gray-white barrier that hovered between them and Joe Wilson. As the clatter of the rotors grew louder, sounded directly overhead, then grew fainter, he silently urged the 'copter to return when the fog lifted. Surely it would lift soon?

His eyes met Moses', saw a shadow settle back on the boy's face. This had to be hardest on Moses, knowing it was his father circling the mountain, probably in serious despair by now. Today was Day Five of being stranded. Jake watched Moses' dark eyes search the cloud cover for long moments, then narrow and fasten on the slope beneath the group. Standing tall on his skis, he pointed his tips downhill and set off even faster than before. Peter quickly leapfrogged ahead of him. Fiona didn't miss a beat catching up with them. Jake was content to stay in sweep position, even if dubiously qualified for it, because he was still unsure about Moses being entirely himself.

Fifteen minutes later, when the light, dry powder beneath him turned into a field of waves headed for a ledge, Jake hesitated. He looked Peter's way, only to note his buddy's eyes blazing with excitement. Peter tossed Jake a smile, centered himself on his board, and accelerated away.

"Uh-oh," Jake thought, gritting his teeth. "Here goes."

10   Action

Peter let the board carry him across the snowfield at gathering speed. For a second, he thought about launching himself off the ledge like in a radical snowboard video, blasting off it in an explosion of powder, grabbing his tail, and hanging for long, effortless seconds. He imagined the film crew catching every gesture against a brilliant blue sky. As he picked up speed, still deciding, everything seemed to go silent. He was suddenly very aware of the crumpling sound of snow flattening beneath the board, the rushing of air in his ears. The lip was frighteningly close. He had no idea what lay below. In an instant, all the magic rushed out of the moment and he had a vision of his legs breaking, his head smashing like a melon over a jagged rock.

His heart in his mouth, he tightened his turn at the last second. Chicken, he thought to himself as his board threw a rooster tail of ice crystals off the cliff. He felt someone watching him. As he stepped out of his bindings and faced Fiona, she turned away and looked over the twenty-foot drop to a rock-infested field of snow through which fog puffs filed like restless cattle in a slaughter yard. She looked determined.

"Fiona, don't do it," he ordered. She continued to study the rocky basin, chin raised, eyes avoiding him.

Jake and Moses pulled up panting. "Quite the cliff. What now?" Moses asked.

"We need to back off and ride along the ridge till we find a way down," Peter replied, voice louder than he intended.

"Look!" Moses said. "Trees. Far side of the gully. Can just see them if you really stare."

Peter turned and squinted through the murky air. Moses might be right; dark silhouettes seemed to hover at the limit of their visible world, like spectators gazing down on a stadium floor. Treeline, and their long-awaited fuel source, if they could just find a way across this cluttered bowl.

"We should go for that chute over there," Peter ruled, pointing left to where the ridge fed a path to the basin floor. "Remember as you're going down to avoid that major boulder in the path, because you won't see it till you're right on top of it. Then slide along that dark shelf — the one at the edge of the bowl beneath a snow overhang — until you're past the rocks and can carve down into the deep snow beyond."

Moses shook his head. "Nope. Get going as fast as you can and get some air off the lip of that boulder. It'll keep you clear of the whole mess of sharp rocks. Then you'll land in the deep powder below. Can't be more than fifteen feet of air."

Peter watched Jake grimace. "I'm going for the technical route through the rocks," Jake offered, lifting his ski pole and spiking it into the snow several times. "As long as I keep turning fast enough, I won't have to take any drops."

Peter studied the route to which Jake was referring. "That's not a bad strategy if you're sure of your turns, Jake. But my board is better suited to traversing the shelf." He blinked at the shelf, wishing it wasn't so deeply shadowed by the overhang.

The silence hung heavy as Peter waited for Fiona to table her cards. Everyone spun around to look at her. To Peter's surprise, she jerked her head in the opposite direction to which they had been pointing.

"See that broken deck?" she asked. They turned to eye a thin rail of snow that straddled the basin a good distance away. A nose of snow off their ridge offered a long-shot jumping platform onto it.

"Looks like it came loose in an avalanche or earthquake," Moses pronounced. "You're not thinking of riding it? It would be a heck of a feat to drop onto it, and a thirty-foot fall if you missed or slipped off it."

Peter shifted his boots back and forth. Should he lay down the law, stop her? Would she listen if he tried to forbid her? Why hadn't he noticed it first, anyway? Doable, maybe. And it would put someone in a good position to pull the rest up the other side of the basin with rope. But, like Moses said, you'd have to be right on the money. Peter shivered, trying to decide how to handle this girl. He'd never met anyone like her, that's for sure. And he knew Jake would be judging his response.

"Peter?" Fiona said, pulling her parka around her. "You're leader. I know I can do it, and then I'll be where you need someone. But it's up to you."

"Fiona …" Jake started to say, but stopped.

Peter spoke in a measured tone. "You've each chosen the routes you feel are best for you. If there's anything I've learned on this trip, it's that everyone here can pull their own weight. So go for it, one at a time, Fiona first, me last. Fiona, transfer the rope from Moses' pack to yours. Everyone's transmitters still on? Okay, see you on the other side."

Peter held his palm out to Fiona. She smiled — possibly the first warm smile he had ever witnessed on her — and slapped his palm with hers. Moses and Jake joined in.

Peter watched Fiona hike her board back up the slope and position herself with care. As Peter's throat tightened — had he made a mistake? — she stepped into her bindings and pushed off. She absorbed the first few bumps with the slightest of knee bends, then shot fast across the snow toward the broad nose. Perfectly centered, and with no twist to her torso, she blazed toward the gap that would land her on the railing.

Peter held his breath. Every muscle in his body locked up. He bit his lower lip as she lofted, floated, and compressed, her eyes fastened on the narrow bridge like they were heat-seeking missiles guaranteed to guide her body to the target. She placed her hands in position the way a pilot extends an airplane's flaps before touchdown. She extended them more as the board hit and slid at high speed along the rail.

Peter felt his fists clench. He felt his body sway as if helping her maintain the grip right to the end. Finally, shoulders held high and not a waver in her body, she slid into the snow at the far side, finishing things off with a last-minute kick.

"Yes!" he screeched, jumping up and down in the snow, giddy with excitement. He grabbed Jake and danced a victory dance. "She aced it."

He couldn't believe he'd let her, couldn't believe he was happy for her, couldn't believe her move in no way tempted him to try the same. How far they had come on this journey.

Moses, face brightening, offered a thumbs-up and executed some power skating to push himself into high gear. Peter frowned as Moses headed for the chute at reckless speed, then forced his mouth into a more positive show of faith. As Moses' skis chattered along the snow, he double-poled a few times to add momentum before tucking and leaping off the top of the boulder overlooking the rock garden. Again, Peter clenched his fists, this time gritting his teeth for good measure. Again, he held his breath. But Moses embraced the air like an eagle and gave them their second iron cross sighting of the day before bringing skis together for the landing. It wasn't a perfect one. One ski hit sooner than the other, and he tottered on his left ski just enough to make Peter's stomach contract. So close to the rocks, Peter thought. So close. But when Moses' arms raised high over his head and he cruised to a finish, Peter and Jake clasped arms around each other.

"You're good?" Peter asked his buddy.

"I'm good to go," Jake answered, zipping his parka up to his chin. "Giant slalom."

With that, Jake headed to the obstacle course that promised no air. Peter watched as he shot down the chute, neatly swishing around Moses' boulder. Then, like an ambitious ball in a pinball game, Jake swiveled his legs left, right, left, right, and left again, keeping his upper body upright and calm. He kept turning with dizzying speed until not a rock was left to dash his skis or body against. He hadn't grazed one.

Peter's turn. He grinned. This was his moment. They were all safe and relaxed now, making their way to the rope Fiona had let down to ease their climb up to treeline. In a moment, while sitting in the darkness of the trees, they would all turn their eyes on him, appraise his every move. He'd done the right thing, letting the others choose their own way. It wasn't how he usually worked, but hey, who said an old guide dog couldn't learn new tricks along the way? Peter felt his chest all but bursting with pride, excitement, happiness. He stepped into his bindings, nodded approvingly as the fog seemed to lift on cue, and waited for the imaginary cameras to begin rolling. Cocking his head toward the chute, he let 'er rip.

Swoosh. The snow parted for his board like a carpet rolling downhill. *Whap! Whap!* He threw in a few switch tricks to rev things up a bit. *Pffft.* He whipped past Moses' boulder with a fancy turn. Frosty air whistled past as the chute dropped away now, hurling itself toward Jake's slalom course. Peter eyed the shelf, studiously ignoring the overhang above it, and tensed all the right muscles — preprogramming each of them to spring for the shelf's darkness at precisely the correct split-second. He felt three pairs of eyes and an army of trees at the forest edge directing their gaze on his perfect acceleration. But just as he arched for the transition, just as he executed his best form ever — carving up onto and tearing along the shadowed shelf — another shadow passed over their bowl. The loud echoing clatter of the rotors drew all eyes away, startled his rhythm, made him jerk in the middle of the high-speed carve-turn designed to feed him to his finish: that patch of deep snow beyond the overhang. He hit it all right, and bang-on where he meant to. But he hadn't figured on hitting it headfirst.

By the time he pulled his head out, the helicopter was gone. Had it seen them? He glanced up to his teammates. Although they were waving wildly, he knew they'd have been hard to see under the trees where they'd gathered. With a sour taste in his mouth, Peter also knew, as silent seconds stretched into mute minutes, that no one, least of all the occupants of the helicopter high above, had glimpsed his ride along the ledge. The helicopter was surely on its way to the boys' original landing point, a place that seemed so very far away now, in more ways than one. A place where everything that could have gone wrong had gone terribly wrong, days — or was it weeks — ago now.

After he had unfurled himself, reached the wall of the bowl directly beneath his buddies, and been pulled up with the rope, Peter lifted his water bottle to his cracked lips. The swallow felt like honey on his scratchy throat, even if only for a second.

He knew that as leader he was supposed to declare this their evening's campsite and order everyone to gather wood for fire. Whether or not a fire would draw rescuers back, they needed to melt snow to reverse the onset of dehydration and cook some food to restore energy and ward off wildlife. He waited for Jake to sound the order, but no one moved or spoke. Finally, Peter observed dryly, "It'll be dark soon. We all know what needs doing."

They did, and in a slow but determined motion, Peter joined them in erecting the tent, gathering firewood, accepting the soup Fiona handed him, and preparing for a good night's sleep.

11 Visitors

The middle of that night, Jake awoke suddenly in the aching cold and darkness, fully alert. He felt around for the pilot's blanket that the four attempted to share over their individual sleeping bags, only to meet Peter's hand doing the same.

"You're awake, too?" his buddy whispered.

"My sore ribs keep me from sleeping for very long at a time."

"I'm sure I've heard wolf howls," Peter said.

Is that what had awakened him? Jake listened intently, ignoring Moses' and Fiona's deep-sleep breathing and the unfamiliar sound of wind-rustled branches. A flash of light momentarily startled him — Peter using his headlamp to check his watch.

"Two a.m.," he whispered. "Do you reckon it's a full wolf pack?"

On cue, the haunting cries sliced through the

frozen night's silence. It started low and mournful, neither far nor near, and crescendoed into a pitch that turned Jake's spine to ice. He reached for Peter's headlamp, not meaning to illuminate Fiona's face as her eyes sprang open and she sat bolt upright. Her eyes grew wide; her hair matted against the door of the tent. One hand reached out to rest on her backpack.

Jake, stepping over Fiona, unzipped the tent door far enough to stick the light out and direct it toward the nearly empty food bag he and Peter had strung high up between two nearby trees earlier that evening.

"What're you doing?" Peter asked him, teeth chattering.

"Checking the food bag. It's fine — well out of reach," Jake said.

"Oh," Fiona said. Jake turned the beam to her, saw her lift her hand from her backpack for a moment, then pause it in mid-air.

"Oh?" Jake said, heart catching, suddenly knowing what she was going to say.

"I … I have some food in my pack. I meant to hand it over before you hung the bag, but you hung it while I was out gathering wood, and I forgot."

A new kind of cold clutched Jake. "Something we can eat quickly right away?" he begged.

"Not really," she whispered. As she turned to unzip her bag with shaking hands, the howls sounded again, much closer, Jake thought with a shudder. He pulled down the zipper of the tent's front door, crawled out a few paces, and grabbed two rocks from the campfire that had long since gone cold. He returned and pulled them into his lap, leaving the tent flap open so he could see whatever needed seeing.

"Wolves?" Jake asked Moses, hoping his voice didn't sound pinched. "Should we go out and start the fire again?"

"Wolves, but they won't hurt us," Moses replied. "It's a myth that wolves attack humans." Jake, thinking that Moses sounded less than certain, watched Peter reach for his backpack and produce the ax, which he gripped by the neck.

"I'll boil some water for tea," Fiona volunteered.

Jake noticed that no one objected, even though it would be the last of their fuel, and even though the tea should have been in the food bag hanging up outside.

By the time her pot had boiled, Moses had extracted two ski poles from the pile outside the tent. Jake played his light around three shivering tentmates. Tension or cold? he wondered.

"Is the tea ready?" he asked Fiona.

"No," she declared, narrowed eyes on the black night outside the tent door.

Jake clicked off the light. That's when he saw them: two tiny orange night lights directly down slope from them — glow-in-the-dark eyes. "A visitor," he announced, more calmly than he felt. He waited, the cold of each rock chilling his palms right through his gloves. The howling had long since stopped. Jake half-wished it would return to offer a clue as to the size and location of the pack behind the orange-eyed leader.

"Scat!" Moses shouted, hurling one of his ski poles out the tent door. The eyes disappeared, but Jake was sure he could hear paws pacing out of sight.

"Tea, please," Peter addressed Fiona, his teeth chattering audibly. Before she could respond, a bulge appeared in the tent wall beside Jake.

"Whoa!" Jake shouted, hurling himself to the other side of the tent and raising one of his rock-filled hands.

Moses drove his second ski pole at the bulge, eliciting a guttural snarl and the sound of paws bolting through the snow. Jake switched his light back on in time to catch a figure starting to head away, then whirling around to face their front door and spitting in their direction. Jake had never seen such a creature. This was no wolf. If anything, it resembled a small brown bear, except for its long bushy tail, terrifyingly large claws, and a stripe running the full length of its body.

"A wolverine!" Moses cried. Peter raised his ax but hesitated as if trying to decide if the creature was going to lunge. That's when Fiona gave it a full face of boiling water at the same time as Jake hit it squarely in the chest with his first missile. The second landed in the snow, because the creature had bolted.

A plaintive cry made Jake shudder all over, but he took comfort in the fact that it sounded farther and farther away.

"Jake," Peter said after a few moments of silence as he set the ax down. "Help me transfer Fiona's food to the food bag outside."

Jake willed his nerves to steady as he crawled out of the tent behind Peter. His body ached with tension as he lowered the rope holding the food bag and, eyes darting everywhere, stuffed the stray food in and raised the bag with shaking hands. Five minutes later, Jake was shivering uncontrollably as he crawled back into the tent, where Moses and Fiona sat clutching the retrieved ski poles.

"Judging from the tracks, she had a little one with her," Jake announced. "Don't think we'll be seeing them again tonight."

He watched Peter turn to Fiona with a smile. "Guess there's no boiled water for tea now. Never mind. Good move. You shoot like you board. Fast and accurate. And I doubt you'll ever keep food in the tent again."

Jake saw Fiona's eyes rise to search Peter's face for signs of sarcasm. Then slowly, her lips produced a smile. Jake watched, amused, as redness crept into Peter's face. His friend leaped into his sleeping bag, zipped it up, and switched off his light.

One light remained on: Jake's, in Fiona's hands. She had tugged a book out of her pack.

"So wolves don't attack, but wolverines do, I take it?" Jake asked Moses.

"Exactly," replied Fiona, holding her book, some kind of wildlife guide. She read aloud: "Wolverine: a fearless, heavy-set mammal with powerful jaws that can crush bones. A poor hunter itself, it tends to follow wolves and bears. Does not hibernate, is active day and night."

"Except after being burned and bruised and having the food it was after strung up," Jake concluded.

Nervous laughter accompanied the crinkling of sleeping bags as Fiona returned her book to her pack and switched off the light. Four sets of hands tugged at the pilot's blanket.

"Good night, everyone," Jake mumbled. "And good fight."

12   Steep and Gnarly

Whoen Jake next awoke, it was from the sound of an ax striking wood. He rolled over and surveyed the sleeping bags beside him to determine who was missing. Peter. Good. They needed firewood. Jake reached for his full water bottle, such a luxury after the past few days. He took a long swig, then rested a hand on his shrunken stomach as the water rumbled down.

"Moses?" he addressed the lumpy sleeping bag beside him. "We should be able to make it down the mountain by dark, right? We can maybe walk right into the twin towns of Pemberton and Mt. Currie by suppertime?"

"Tonight or tomorrow, yes, assuming no problems, which is saying something, given our record," Moses said quietly. "We'll run out of food today. After that, we live off our fat, and even though I've got the advantage there, let's hope we're back to civilization soon. All that's really important is we have water now. And an ax and trees to melt more whenever we need it."

"So what's ahead of us today?" Jake pressed.

"Never skied this side of the mountain."

"But you've seen it from the air."

"Yeah. So? It's not like I was picking out ski routes at the time." Moses grinned.

"But what did it look like?"

Moses sighed. "Okay, it's probably going to get steep and gnarly in places. We'll just have to go easy."

"And?"

"I s'pose we'll get to patchy snow and mud around two thousand feet above Pemberton — meaning we'll be removing our skis and boards and walking at some point."

Jake let the silence stretch, wanting something more from Moses, but hesitant to ask. "Moses …" he finally ventured, just as Peter crawled back into the tent.

"No," Moses smiled.

"But I haven't asked yet."

"But you and Peter are doing just fine. You're both natural-born leaders. Anyway, I'm not getting between you more than I already have. And like I said, I don't know this side of the mountain."

Jake drummed his fingers on his sleeping bag, sat

up, and looked at Moses sternly. "Forget Peter's prickliness. You've seen this bit from the air, you're a good skier, your instincts are good, and it's your turn to lead. I'm still not back to full strength."

Moses rolled over in his sleeping bag and sighed. Jake got the sense Moses' eyes were avoiding Peter's.

"Leave him alone," Peter spoke up. "He doesn't have to lead."

Jake ignored Peter. "Moses, you say I'm a natural leader. But you know what a good leader's supposed to do? Create more leaders. You want to know why you'd be our best leader today? 'Cause you know more than all of us put together about the backcountry, especially here, even if it's not everything your grandfather knew. And because it's your instincts that have been keeping us alive."

Moses flipped back toward Jake, then looked to Peter, whose eyes narrowed and mouth tightened. But Peter said nothing. Fiona busied herself with the stove. Before Peter or Moses could speak, Jake, who'd made up his mind, extended his hand to Moses. When Moses didn't take it, he punched Moses softly on his shoulder as if it was a done deal, shed his sleeping bag, and headed out the tent door for the food bag.

When he returned, he allowed his eyes to meet Moses'. Expressionless as always. Or maybe not. Jake was getting better by the day at reading Moses, and he could've sworn a smile was hiding in the crinkles around Moses' eyes.

"Deal," Moses said solemnly. They ate their reconstituted powdered beef stroganoff in silence, then lined up their water bottles to fill with the water Fiona had just boiled.

"Steep and gnarly today, kids," Moses said at length. "I'll lead off, but when the trees get thick and the slope gets steep, pair up, keep calling out to each other to keep in contact, and leapfrog each other slowly. I'll take Fiona as partner. For now, Peter should sweep. I'll change off with him later."

"Do we need transmitters?" Fiona ventured.

Her words made Jake's throat catch. Any memory, however fleeting, of the helicopter crash and avalanche still pained him. It wasn't a memory he could deal with yet. And he certainly wasn't going to let it pull him back into the scary numbness he'd only just fought his way out of yesterday.

"Yes, Fiona, we still need transmitters," he ruled.

"What about sticking around here for the day and building up a fire to attract rescuers?" Peter asked.

Jake looked to Moses. Peter frowned.

"Sixth day out, no guarantee there'll be planes or helicopters today," Moses said. "And not easy for them to see us or land below treeline anyway. We're not many hours from getting down the mountain. We're all good skiers and boarders. I say go for it. There're sticky cinnamon buns waiting for us in Mt. Currie."

Jake smiled. Fiona smiled. Peter tossed his bag out the tent, then collapsed it for packing. Jake, wondering why Peter was in a rotten mood, joined him in rolling up the tent. Soon, all four were gathered near the skis and boards stuck in a nearby snowbank.

Moses kicked off without a word. For the next hour or two, Jake enjoyed skiing beside Peter as Moses carved safe routes between the trees without getting too far ahead. The brilliant blue sky and warm sun lit up a dazzling layer of crystals. The trees, scattered sentries at first but crowding ever closer as the group descended, poked branches out from elegant white robes that glittered in the morning light. Soft white peaks marched endlessly in every direction, a gathering of magnificent giants. The panorama took Jake's breath away. Even the snow was perfection itself: feathery-light powder. "White gold," his father used to call it on family ski outings when Jake was young.

"Peter, watch my line," Jake shouted, leapfrogging past his partner playfully and slaloming through a lineup of half a dozen trees.

"No sweat," Peter responded, jumping into action when Jake paused and tracing the same path with a little jump in the middle for effect. As Peter drew up to Jake, Jake felt a light touch on his back. "You're it. Catch me if you can," Peter taunted.

In and out of trees they wound, chasing, laughing, searching out mogul-like bumps, occasionally catching an edge and tumbling into the snow. Sometimes they could hear Moses and Fiona up ahead doing much the same.

Here and there the descent sped up, working Jake's sweat glands while inspiring Peter to crank high-speed turns or lay in some radical cuts that nearly flipped him over. Here and there, the slope would grow more gradual, allowing Jake to breathe in the fresh air and drink in the alpine views, while Peter — so he said — would go searching for the elusive perfect lip and pile of powder for performing his first-ever backflip. Once, Peter's brazen antics landed him in a tree well, prompting Jake to rush over and pull him out.

"Good thing we partnered up," Jake chided him.

"Let's do synchronized ski-boarding," Peter challenged in return, linking a few turns. Jake smiled and responded with a sloppy pirouette that didn't quite plant his face in the snow.

"Whoo-hoo," Peter enthused. "We're hot!" He attempted a big-air jump between two slopes, but as he fishtailed on the far side and began to slide backwards, he was forced to throw all his weight to one side and execute a 180-degree flip. Quickly converting that into a downhill slide, he finished, winked, and said, "Your turn."

Jake rubbed his chin, thought hard how to answer that move on skis, then raced up to a snow hump, launched himself off, and did a perfect 360 with a smooth landing.

"Wow," Peter said. Half an hour after that, he started leaping up and down. "I found it, Jake. I found it. It's sweet. It's perfect. It's all mine."

"What have you found, Peter?" Jake asked dryly, never quite sure whether to encourage Peter's craziness.

"My backflip drop. Been waiting forever. I'm going to do it, buddy. I'm going to."

"'Perfect' meaning a broad lip, a landing soft as a trampoline, and no Fiona to giggle if you make a fool of yourself?"

Peter blushed big-time; Jake enjoyed every second of it.

"I said I'm going to do it. It's what I've been wait-ing half my life for, Jake old buddy. Just watch."

Jake turned to study the terrain Peter was so excited about. Sure enough, a natural ramp with a thick lip looked almost enticing, like a bunny hill looks to a novice. Jake had seen plenty of backflips on videos. Those guys always made it look easy, and why wouldn't they, since the video makers edited out the crashes that took guys to hospitals? Or showed the crashes all in one concentrated spot for those who liked gore. But Peter was Peter, and who was Jake to discourage him from taking a long leap off a short ramp? It was sunny and Peter said it was perfect. That was good enough for Jake. A formation brought to you by nature and custom-designed for a first back-flip. Heck, Peter was unstoppable at the best of times, let alone when hyped to this level.

"I'm watching, Peter."

Peter slid toward the ramp, picked up speed, and launched without a flicker of hesitation. Up curved his board, up curved Peter in a neat swoop behind it. Playing the crisp air like an invisible half-pipe, he swung up, up until his head was pointing at the ground. Then he just as smoothly drew the rest of the circle against the blue, blue sky and tucked for the landing. It wouldn't have won a gold medal. He wobbled at the end and had to jerk his hands about to maintain his balance. But he finished on his feet, face as brilliantly happy as Jake had ever witnessed.

"Yes, yes, yes, yes, yes!" he enthused so loudly that a raven took sudden flight from a nearby tree.

"Yes," Jake agreed. "You're the man. You showed us how it's done. And thank goodness I don't have to explain to your mom and dad why I had to haul you down the last bit of the mountain on a makeshift backboard."

Peter guffawed at that. "So, ski-partner. Can you match that one?"

"I give up. You win," Jake said, slapping him on the back and letting Peter's wide grin infect his own. "Enough play, though. I'm off to make sure our other partners are okay. We do want to be down this mountain before dark. And it's lunchtime. Or should I say midday, since lunch isn't a happening thing any more?"

"Tell me about it," Peter said, rubbing his stomach.

Jake chose a line well clear of Peter's ramp and let his skis accelerate downhill. Soon he found himself weaving through a thick stand of trees. His pulse quickened as the only navigable route tapered to a track too narrow for turns. Battling to slow down, he felt the icy touch of panic tap the back of his throat as he flew faster and faster, hemmed in by darkening walls of trees on both sides.

Should he risk a fall or play it out? Every second added speed, making a deliberate fall less inviting. But the thought of smashing into a tree terrified him, made his ribs hurt just thinking about it. His knees were turning to oatmeal, his body shuddered with each bump absorbed, his stomach was a bubbling science experiment ready to fizz over.

"Surrender," his brain commanded. That helped somewhat, made him try to go with the flow. If he had no plan, maybe the spillway down which he was barreling did. It did indeed. With no warning, it ended in a dip, which launched him into the air.

"Yiiiii!" he screamed, trying to keep skis together, breathe, and snatch a peek at his destiny below all at the same time.

"Surrender," the mountain whispered as he flew over some downed trees and headed for a snowbank. *Thud*. For the second time in a week, Jake demonstrated a live burial. But as burials went, this one was rather pleasant. Not unlike being whacked from both sides at once with pillows. He landed kind of like a cheerleader demonstrating, "Gimme a 'Y!'"

He'd have been happy to stay there for the afternoon, seated in his snug new snow seat, if an image of Peter landing on top of him hadn't flashed across the inside of his closed eyelids. That's when he rolled to his side, just in time for Peter to drop beside him, backside first, deepening the soft snow pile's considerable dent.

Jake rolled back upright and blinked as his shoulder touched Peter's. They looked at each another, then looked up. Jake gazed at their legs, sticking up like four straws in a snow cone, Peter's locked together by his board. As they looked at each other again, what started as snickers built into howls of laughter. Jake's body, so stiff and terrified seconds before, convulsed from the sheer silliness of the situation, releasing every droplet of tension he'd stored up the last few days.

By the time Moses' and Fiona's curious faces appeared at the edge of their crater, the two were spent. Wiping tears from his eyes, trying to wipe the dumb grin off his face, Jake unclipped his skis and accepted Moses' hand up out of the snowbank's new dimple.

"Hey," he panted a little as he settled himself on the edge of the rim. "Soft landing, but could've been bad."

"Could've," Moses agreed with a smile. "It's Peter's turn to lead now."

"No worries," Peter responded, accepting Moses' and Jake's extended palms. With one strong tug, they helped Peter rise from the mound's center.

"Looky here," Peter said, slapping snow off his snow pants as he gazed down the slope. "If that isn't the sweetest sight for sore eyes, I sure don't know what is."

13   Ghost Town

"**Y**ou mean the road?" Fiona asked. "Moses and I were just trying to figure out if that's what it is."

"Definitely a road," Peter said, elated. "What do you think, Jake? Logging? A cabin? Either way, it will get us down quickly."

"For sure," Jake agreed.

Peter pushed off toward the sun-soaked space. Man, was he hungry. He visualized a cabin stocked with canned food. He'd never been good at going from one meal to the next without snacks, let alone going one day to the next without a meal. Oh well; he needed to look at it as part of the adventure and risk of backcountry sports. What a story they'd have to relate to everyone when they made it back to Joe's heliport. For sure they'd get written up in all the Canadian papers. Even the Seattle papers would run this story. "Four kids survive avalanche, crevasse, and journey down a mountain." Hmmm, how about "Seattle boy guides three companions out of Canadian wilderness"? Just kidding. Let's see. "Mountain disasters prove teens' mettle." Yeah, that was good. Maybe he should get a job writing newspaper headlines.

He glanced up and noticed that their perfect day was deteriorating. A thin bank of fog had crept up the mountain toward them. He halted, stared at what looked like a clearing and shouted, "Guys! Come 'ere."

Jake, Moses, and Fiona joined him. Peter powered down the path, then pulled a jubilant jump. "Look! Buildings!" His heart leaped. He'd hoped for a cabin but certainly hadn't expected a large cluster of buildings. Maybe there were people here who could help them. People with vehicles, radios, telephones, food. He burst into the clearing with gusto, then paused. Wisps of white floated around him as if examining him with malicious intent. It was too quiet here. The rutted road hadn't been used in many years. And the buildings were in terrible disrepair, windows with shards of glass offering dark openings into dead and rotting buildings, doors long since fallen from their frames.

Peter rounded a corner and gazed up at the largest of the buildings, which stepped down a steep, stump-covered slope like a hunchbacked giant on elbows and knees, its corrugated tin roof patches curled back in places.

"An old mine," he said, and shivered.

Moses, Jake, and Fiona pulled up behind him.

"Old Ryan Mine," Moses said at length. "Operated in the early to mid-1900s. Said to be haunted."

"Haunted?" Fiona asked.

"Haunted by a miner who was killed in his sleep with an ax by another miner who thought he'd stolen his gold poke. A poke was a purse. Can't remember anything else of the story," Moses said. "We must be at around four-thousand-foot elevation now. The snow will start getting soft soon."

"There's the tunnel," Jake said, pointing to a dark opening framed by rock into which was inscribed, "1918." Twisted rails ran out from the tunnel, which was half-blocked by a cart with peeling yellow paint on its metal frame, rotted-wood sides and bottom, and rusted wheels indented to run along the tracks.

Peter registered a steady drip-drip sound from inside that reminded him of the crevasse. He shivered as a whisper of air movement, warmer than the outside air temperature, prickled the hairs on his face and carried a hint of minerals to his nose.

"Let's drop our packs, skis, and boards here and explore," he suggested. "Look for food, vehicles, or a caretaker."

"Not necessarily in that order," Jake added with a grin.

"Who wants to explore the big mine building with me?" Peter asked.

"Me," Moses said.

"Sounds good. Fiona and I will check out the cabins," Jake offered.

Even though he was keen to get down the mountain, Peter was also dying to look inside the main building, the mill several stories high with hundreds of broken windows. Just for a minute or two.

He and Moses trotted quietly through the snow and fog, like ghosts entering another era. Caretaker? Not likely. This place hadn't been visited for a very long time. An ax murder? Now that was spooky. Good thing he didn't believe in ghosts, Peter thought.

Peter reached the building first. The door creaked long and loud with a mere touch. Before them was a cement platform with an impressive array of rusted iron: mucking machines, flatbeds, hoppers, carts, wheels, and machinery all lying askew. Beyond the platform was a set of rotted wooden stairs without benefit of a railing. They stretched far and away upward, beside a steep set of iron rails, not unlike a roller coaster ride. Whatever the miners had been mining must have been sent down in the wagons.

Neither Peter nor Moses spoke as they craned their

necks to see where the stairs led. It looked like they ended in a tiny office at the top rear of the building.

"I'm going up," Peter announced. Moses didn't object. Testing each board first with a little pressure from his toes, sometimes stretching his legs to lift himself over a series of missing or collapsed planks, Peter climbed. Moses was right behind him.

Halfway up, Peter turned to look down. Bad idea. His knees began to shake. He hated heights. Plus, shadows lurked, the smell of neglect and decay filled his nostrils, and the steps seemed ever less trustworthy. He lifted his eyes to the little office at the top. Supervisor's place. Kind of like the media box hung high over a big indoor sports arena, except that most of the windows were broken. Bird's-eye view of the operation. Must have been something seventy-five, a hundred years ago. If he kept his eyes on that, he'd be okay, he decided. He carried on, Moses puffing behind.

Up in the office, two old chairs and a beaten-up wood desk beckoned. The boys plunked down on the wooden seats in which vandals had carved initials, and put their feet up as if they were invited guests waiting for their host to appear.

"Don't mind Jake. He's always been a little bossy," Peter said, running his finger along the desk and inspecting the dust it collected.

"Guess you've known him longer than me," Moses

replied, shifting in the seat and jumping when it squeaked.

"When you don't feel like leading, just let him know," Peter advised Moses.

"I do. But you need to take your turn without undermining him when it's his turn, Peter. And let me take mine without feeling like I'm between the two of you. If I'm allowed to return advice, that is."

Peter drew squiggles in the dust on the desk's surface, checked his watch. Definitely time to change the subject. "You going to be a helicopter pilot like your dad?" he asked Moses abruptly.

Moses tipped back in his office chair, studied a loose ceiling board, placed his hands behind his head. "That's what *he* wants. It's all he ever talks about. I don't want to do that."

Peter studied the ink-stained surface of the table in front of them. "But you do want to go to college, right? Don't you want to get off your reserve, train to do something interesting?"

"I have a few friends who live to get off the reserve, but I want to stay there, be someone who makes it a better place, be a teacher maybe. It's my community."

"That's great," Peter offered, unsure what else to say.

"I'm into languages. I'm good at French, and I'm studying Yinka Déné, my native language, with an elder."

"Oh," said Peter. "Your native tongue. But isn't that a dead language? Why would you want to study something no one speaks any more? Spanish or German or Mandarin will get you a good job, if you're good at languages."

Moses stood and shuffled about the office, peered through a broken window at the mill floor far below. "Languages are more than words, Peter. They're cultures. They're pride. They're keys to things almost lost. I can't believe I'm even telling you any of this stuff. I hardly know you."

"How can you hardly know someone you've been stuck on a mountain with for six scary days? We'd recognize each others' body odor from a mile away by now."

Moses smiled and sat down. "What're you doing after high school, Mr. Montpetit? You going to be a pilot like your dad?"

"Thought you'd never ask. Haven't decided between being an actor and a sports broadcaster."

"Let's see, a sports broadcaster has to talk loud and fast, and a lot. Has to be kind of hyperactive."

"And handsome, don't forget. A take-charge sort of leader." Peter winked. "You and Fiona have stuff in common, you know. She wants to be a doctor in Third World countries, you're into your community, and the two of you both speak dead languages. Hers is deader," he added with a smirk. "Guess we've had our look-see here. No food or caretakers. Let's go find Jake and Fiona."

Before they could rise, Peter noticed Moses stiffen and place his finger to his lips. Peter froze and listened. He heard a step creak far below them. Jake must be coming to see what was keeping them. But something stopped Peter from calling out.

Creak. There it was again, higher up the flight of ancient stairs. Reluctantly, Peter admitted that Jake wouldn't creep up without shouting out first.

Slowly, Moses rose, just enough to peak out a filthy portion of glass still in the office window. Peter watched Moses' face, thought it blanched a little, and lifted his own bottom off the chair just enough to peer out beside Moses. It's not what he saw. It's what he didn't see.

There was nothing and no one on the stairs.

"Let's get out of here," Moses whispered.

14   Wheels

"**P**eter, Moses!" Jake called out as he saw his buddies emerge from the big building. He galloped as fast as one can gallop in stiff ski boots and grabbed Peter and Moses by the shoulders. "You won't believe what we've just found."

Moses and Peter just stared at him blankly, their faces a little white.

"Two all-terrain vehicles in a shed! Mud-covered and old but …"

"Petrol in them," Fiona joined in.

"She means gas," Jake said. "Gas in 'em! Three-wheelers!" He watched Peter's eyes widen.

"No keys in the ignition? And no one around?"

Jake let a grin break right across his face. "That's right, no one around. Keys? Who needs keys? Am I not a whiz mechanic's son? Sam's Adventure Tours' ace fix-it man? Think I don't know how to hot-wire a simple little machine like an ATV? Are we ever in luck!"

"Jake," Fiona broke in from behind, "I don't want to sound stupid, but ATVs aren't exactly common in my neighborhood in London. So I need to ask, aren't they for dirt roads? Will they run on snow? Could they be dangerous if we do get them started?"

"*If* we can get them started?" Jake flushed. "Fiona, we want down this mountain, right? And we've just been handed two vehicles to take us directly there. Food, parents, warm beds, everything, are just an hour away now." He couldn't believe she was questioning him.

"Wait." Peter stepped forward. "I don't want to pop your balloon, Jake, but Fiona is right. They're not going to drive well on snow, especially on a warm day like today, at this elevation where things are starting to get soft. They'll slide around on us if they don't sink outright."

"I agree," Moses said.

"See? Moses agrees," Peter said cheerfully. Jake was totally floored. "So here's what we're going to do," Peter continued. "We're going to take strips of the corrugated tin roof lying around here and jury-rig a snowmobile-like ski under the front tire."

Jake watched one head nod after another, observed Peter drink in the way everyone was staring at him. Peter-the-leader. Jake smiled.

"How about using the snowboards instead?" Jake asked.

Peter and Fiona put their hands on their hips in perfect synch.

"Dream on," came the forceful British accent.

"Never mess with a redhead," Peter added with a wink.

Ten minutes later, the shed that Jake and Fiona had found buzzed with activity.

"Enough yet?" Moses asked, dragging in his fifth strip of tin and dropping it at Peter's feet.

"One of these is okay. Need another this size," Peter directed.

"Jake, can you toss me those wire cutters?" Fiona asked as she unrolled a spool of wire for Peter.

"Sorry, not now," Jake mumbled, stomach sprawled on the driver's seat of one of the ATVs, head in the engine compartment, jumper wires in hand. "Yes!" he shouted, a few minutes of fiddling later.

Hands clapped as the first sputter sounded. Jake revved it up gradually to the cadence of a live if reluctant engine. Hardly had Jake disentangled himself from his uncomfortable position when Peter and Moses disengaged the tire to make sure it wouldn't spin while on its ski, and positioned themselves on each side to lift the front end just enough for Fiona to slide the ski under. After stringing the wire to the parts Peter suggested, she stepped back, tossed her mane of hair back and said, "Next on the assembly line, please."

As Jake coaxed the second ATV to grumble to life, his three teammates all but jumped on him for a spontaneous hug. Not unlike a winning pit crew, Jake decided. Peter, pit crew boss, was positively gloating.

"Two limos, four bodies," Jake declared. "Who are the drivers?"

"You and Peter, of course," Fiona said, wiping her hands on a dirty curtain hanging across the shed's window. "I don't know how to drive on the right side of the road anyway."

Jake was surprised when Peter looked to Moses. "Do you want the honors?" Peter asked.

Moses hesitated. "Don't mind if I do," he decided.

"Our gear!" Fiona called out. "It's back at the tunnel!"

"First stop, tunnel," Jake announced as he leaped into the first machine's driver's seat and waited for Peter to sling his legs over and perch awkwardly behind. Jake felt the machine leap at his command. He grinned till he thought his face would split as the machine roared and banked any way he asked it. But when they pulled up to the tunnel, Jake stared. Not a single item was there. He looked left, looked right. He studied the snow, saw only their tracks. He turned to see Peter and Moses exchange glances.

"The packs! The skis! The snowboards!" he exclaimed. "They're gone!" No one replied.

Jake peered around. The fog had lifted a little, not entirely. Wispy forms of mist still moved in creepy layers between the silent buildings.

"So is the ax," Fiona observed.

"Don't say it like that," Moses said. "Don't even think it. I don't believe in ghosts. Especially ax-murderer ghosts."

"Ghost, hermit, hippie, squatter, vagrant. Whoever stole our stuff is now armed and dangerous. It's someone I don't want to meet. Let's get out of here," Jake said.

Vroom! Vroom! And they were off, the din seeming to frighten the fog into lifting some more.

Jake loved the power beneath him, loved the way the ATV handled. The back wheels sank a bit in the warm snow, it was true, but the ski kept the thing going forward. Good idea, that. Jake tugged on the wheel, smiled as it swerved a little. Nice. He'd have loved to go full throttle, swing it dangerously around corners, but, well, it was snow, and he was just getting the feel of it, and after everything else they'd been through, they didn't need an ATV rollover. So he let the beast putter along like a sissy golf cart.

Half an hour later, he found himself drumming his gloves on the side of the fuel tank. This was boring.

The strain of holding the ATV back from what it was meant to do was weighing even on his cautious nature.

"Come on," Peter shouted from behind, as if reading Jake's mind. He clapped his hands on Jake's shoulders. "Let 'er go!"

Moses beat him to it. With a rev as loud as a chainsaw, the youth lurched past Jake with a smile and a wave. Jake glimpsed Fiona lean forward and clutch Moses' waist for dear life. Her flying red hair failed to cover her smile.

Vroom, vroom. Jake applied a full handful of throttle and rounded a corner with slippery finesse.

"Yahoo!" Peter shouted in his ear. "Come on, you old grandma!"

Jake strained for a sighting of Moses, couldn't believe the boy had accelerated out of sight already. Jake knew he shouldn't push it, knew the twisty old mining road might hold surprises, but hey, he wasn't going to sit still and be called a grandma. He gripped the wheel and leaned into the next curve. Peter all but fell into him, then circled arms around his chest and laughed like a madman.

"That's the way, Jake! Knew you had it in you!"

Jake's jaw rotated as he pulled the vehicle out of a fishtail and tightened as he whipped it around the end of a fallen tree. He hunched his shoulders forward and rolled a fistful of throttle as a steep straightaway appeared and the back wheels of Moses' vehicle shot out of sight around a corner.

"Wheeee!" Peter provided sound effects. Trees blurred past, shuddering at the noise, dropping snow loads from their branches in protest. Crows, ravens, and little whisky-jacks took to the air.

As he plunged down the steep grade and careened left to take a corner, Jake panicked when he saw Moses and Fiona stopped in the center of the road. He backed off his throttle hold, but it was too late. He squeezed the brakes, leaned toward the middle of the road, fighting its slide to the edge. He heard Peter scream as the machine's right side lifted high into the air and slung him out. Jake fought against tipping out as the ATV teetered. Then it slammed down, ski defining the edge of the road, one back wheel still on the road, one dangling high over a drop-away, over the receding fog.

Jake, hardly daring to move, leaned instinctively to his left toward the road. Peter was lying full-length on it. Moses and Fiona were on foot, sprinting toward them.

"Don't move," Moses shouted to Jake as Fiona bent over Peter.

Moses planted his feet in the snow and extended an arm to Jake.

Jake, still in a daze, took it, and leaped out of the vehicle just as it tottered, then rolled down the slope.

"Close one," Moses said.

"Phew," Peter said, leaping up before Fiona could touch him. "That could have been us."

"I braked to keep from crashing into you," Jake said, hand pressing on his thumping heart as he looked at Moses. "Why did you stop in the middle of the road like that?" He'd never imagined ATVs were so tippy, snow or not.

"Out of petrol," Fiona said.

"Gas," Moses clarified.

"Oh." Jake shook himself, eyed Peter, who looked fine, and peered over the road edge where the ATV had gone. It sat bottom-up quite a distance down.

"Doesn't look damaged, wouldn't be too hard to bring up with the right equipment, but *we'd* have been damaged if we'd gone down with it," Jake ruled with a tremor in his voice. He ordered himself to straighten his shoulders and sound natural. "So, we're down to walking. Can't be far." He surveyed the purple haze of the valley just below, still covered by a smattering of fog.

"Sorry, Peter. I got carried away, was going a bit too fast to stop easily, and it was them or us."

"Well, I'll remember that next time," Peter teased. "It was a heck of a ride, anyway."

Jake shivered. He shouldn't have been going quite so fast. But Peter was right. It had been a heck of a ride. As they plodded along the road, Jake's ribs and ankle throbbed. Too little food, too much stress and exercise, too many days. Had it really been only six days since the helicopter had dropped them off so innocently at ten thousand feet? Nancy and Sam must be in a terrible state. His mother and Alyson, Peter's parents, everyone. Even Search and Rescue.

Weakened as they were, though, they were alive, and probably very close now to a human settlement. They were alive and uninjured, save for Jake's bruised ribs and ankle, entirely due to their own resourcefulness and determination. And none of them were the same people who'd sat at that sticky-bun café six days ago.

As his boots crunched through the wet snow, Jake reflected that Moses had been unafraid of taking the lead today on the ATV, especially since Peter had encouraged him. Peter was being more responsible — well, except for on the ATV ride. Fiona was smiling way more than when they'd met her, and seemed comfortable with everyone at last. And himself? Jake smiled. He'd cheated death at least once. And if holding these characters together as a team for six days was worth anything, there must be a job waiting for him at the United Nations. Jake Evans, diplomat, mediator, shrink. Those are all part of leadership, he knew now. His dad would be proud of him, and maybe that's all that mattered.

But they weren't home yet, and Jake had had his fill of walking in ski boots. Clomping across a parking lot to a ski lift in these things was tolerable, but hiking down a mountain was just not on. His feet would be a mass of angry blisters by Pemberton. Knees and ankles ached in harmony with his ribs. Even the knowledge that nothing was likely to thwart them from their destination now failed to energize his steps. It was just one foot in front of another. Until, that is, Fiona began to sing Latin choir songs again. Positively exotic on this snow-covered road amid lodgepole pine and hemlock spruce trees and the occasional caw of a black raven or crow. He was glad she kept it up, mile after mile, gradually lifting their spirits, until interrupted by the noise of a vehicle approaching.

Afraid it might be a mirage, certain it would turn around if they didn't catch it, Jake broke into a run, the others on his heels. But just as the shiny red snowmobile came into view, it swerved to take a fork in the road.

"Help!" Jake shouted, sprinting faster toward the plume of snow, as if the driver would hear them over the deafening roar of the machine.

They took the same fork at a trot, relieved to see the snowmobile stop within sight. But by the time they reached the machine, it was empty. They followed the driver's footprints along a trail. Jake's jaw dropped a few moments later when they rounded a corner to see a man wearing nothing but a cowboy hat and boxers, cowboy boots in his hands.

"What the h—?" the man shouted as he glimpsed the four of them. Jake reckoned they must look pretty strange, indeed. Four kids in ski and snowboard gear, no skis or boards to be seen. But who was weirder, them or this kook?

The grizzled man scratched his head and stared. "Where in blazes did you folks come from?"

Jake watched Fiona's eyes grow large as she surveyed his pile of clothing in the snow. "And what kind of party is *this?*" Jake inquired with a twisted smile.

"Hey, this is the middle of nowhere, and everyone goes in the hot springs buck naked," the cowboy answered, winking at Fiona, who drew back a step.

Jake swiveled his head to notice, for the first time, steam rising from behind a nearby mound, and a rivulet of warm water trickling nearby. Hot springs? Nice. But relaxing wasn't topmost on his mind.

"Got any food in your snowmobile?" Jake asked. Food first. Explanations later.

The cowboy stared and scratched his head. "Beer

and peanuts. I'm Stuart, by the way. Stuart Jay. Say, you aren't those kids that got killed in a helicopter crash and avalanche, are you? Well, I'll be damned."

The peanuts disappeared faster than Stuart could produce them from a storage compartment in his snowmobile. As for the beer, it stayed there as four male bodies plunked themselves into the hot springs. Fiona turned her back politely as the others got settled, then rolled up the legs of her thermals to go in no further than her knees.

The cowboy said nothing more for half an hour as the four took turns telling him their story and appreciating the warmth and relaxation of soaking stiff muscles in the pool.

"Well, I'll be damned," he said again when they'd finished. "And to think you got taken by Crazy Collin."

"Who?" Jake asked.

"Crazy Collin, been livin' up at the mine for years, never shows his face to anyone except when he comes to town to buy stuff at the grocery or hardware store. Bet he was pleased as a peacock to get a free ax and shovels, and you can count on those skis and boards showing up at his sister's next yard sale. Unless, of course, we tell O'Toole, Pemberton's RCMP man, to go fetch 'em before then."

"But there were no tracks in the snow where we left the stuff, except ours," Jake insisted.

Stuart laughed a full-bodied laugh, gold teeth glinting like nuggets in a gold pan. "That Collin's good. You aren't the first visitors to be had, y'know. He's a runt of a man, Crazy Collin is, smaller than Fiona here, and he's got the habit of stepping in other people's tracks so he doesn't make any himself. Clever little weasel, he is. But harmless as a shadow. And you got him back by takin' his ATVs for a spin.

"Anyhow, time to get you kids back to your moms and dads before your memorial services are over. You'll be quite the sensation, you know. Wish I had a cellphone to offer you, but I spent my wad on my machine. Lift, anyone? Pile on best you can. First stop, we pick up my sister. She's the Pemberton correspondent for the Whistler newspaper and if this isn't a scoop, I never seen one! Then direct to Joe's heliport. He'll come running outta there at record-breakin' speed."

As the four youths filed quietly to Stuart's snowmobile, Jake paused to look up at the mountain. The others stopped as if wanting to say their goodbyes to it, too.

"*Veni, vidi, vici,*" Fiona whispered.

"Hey," Peter said. "I know that Latin. Comes from Julius Caesar, the Roman emperor. We came, we saw, we conquered."

Moses turned and smiled at Fiona. "No," he objected.

"*Dzulh tsa nazya. Dzulh h ona dilh e. Dzulh ne na chalh ya.* We came, and the mountain taught and changed us."

"And we'll take those lessons to our next adventure," Jake promised softly.

15 Yellow Ribbons

The Whistler Question, May 29

Teens lost on mountain found alive!
*Pemberton ranch hand discovers
"half-starved" kids at hot springs*
By Esther Jay

Dateline: Pemberton, British Columbia

Days into a Search and Rescue air search for four missing teens thought killed in an avalanche, the three boys and one girl showed up alive with only mild injuries at a hot springs off Pemberton Mountain road.

Discovered by Pemberton ranch hand Stuart Jay, the young survivors — including the 15-year-old son of Joe Wilson, who runs Eagle Heli-Ski Tours out of

Mt. Currie and was involved in the search — are reported to be in good condition.

"They were half-starving and missing their gear, but in mint shape, considering," Jay reports. "I knew right away who they were, fed them what I had, then drove them to Mt. Currie, where their families were waiting. It was some reunion. Lots of tears."

"We're overwhelmed and overjoyed," said Nancy Sheppard, manager of Sam's Adventure Tours in Chilliwack, which had contracted Wilson to fly the junior guides up to Lillooet Glacier for a heli-ski and snowboard training trip. "We just can't believe it. And we're so thankful to all the people of the Pemberton/ Mt. Currie area who have helped search for them the past week." Sheppard is acting as spokesperson for the parents and children, who have declined media interviews.

"They're exhausted and hungry, but thrilled to be safe. The families need some privacy right now as they reunite after this trauma, and we ask the media to respect that."

Outside the Pemberton motel where the families are holed up, dozens of reporters are gathered, and well-wishers have delivered mountains of flowers and cards. Meanwhile, the townspeople of the twin towns of Pemberton and Mt. Currie have been decking their communities with yellow ribbons since the news broke.

Details are sketchy, but Sheppard said three of the 15-year-olds had wilderness safety training, which helped them survive their ordeal. One survived the Extreme Adventure Tours helicopter crash last week. The other three rescued her. Trapped by last week's record-breaking storm, the four experienced an avalanche, a harrowing escape from a crevasse, a wolverine attack, and a near-crash on all-terrain vehicles, Sheppard said. "They built snow caves twice and demonstrated outstanding judgement and determination throughout."

Jay said the group suffered the theft of their gear on the way down but received it back last night. He declined to offer further details. No charges are being laid.

The Pemberton Search and Rescue office, which coordinated an intensive search involving many volunteers from the district, says it will issue a statement tomorrow, after getting more information from the teens and their families.

"Many hours and resources were put into the search. We're obviously very relieved that these young people have been found alive and safe, and we hope to have more details shortly," spokesperson Grant Granovski told a news conference.

Granovski has confirmed that two staff members of Mt. Currie's Extreme Adventure Tours, pilot

Jonathan Mathew and guide Sean Neal, were killed instantly when their helicopter crashed on Monday. Their bodies have not yet been recovered from the avalanche that the crash triggered. Their families have been notified but could not be reached for comment.

The survivors' names are Jake Evans of Chilliwack, Peter Montpetit of Seattle, Moses Wilson of Prince George, and Fiona Kerton of London, England.

Acknowledgements

Above all, I'm indebted to Ian Taylor, MD, Search and Rescue volunteer, skier, mountaineer, and friend. Special thanks to Lars Andrews, mountain guide; Curtis Foreman, snowboard "action consultant"; Deb Jones, ski instructor; Jim Cooper, helicopter pilot; and Kristen Clausen of the B.C. Museum of Mining. Three First Nations writers were generous enough to read the manuscript and offer feedback: Diane Silvey, Larry Loyie, and Joanne MacDonald. Also, thanks to April Ingham of the First People's Cultural Foundation in Victoria, B.C.; Marlene Erickson, director of the Yinka Déné Institute of Prince George (www.ydli.org) and the College of New Caledonia, B.C.; and translators Armand Sam and Dr. William Poser. And a special tribute to Margaret Gagnon, one of fewer than six elders who speak the Lheidli dialect of Yinka Déné. She is so committed to preserving her language and culture that she taught until she could no longer get out of bed. Then, to help with a language documentation project, she had workers interview and record her from her bed for forty-five minutes twice a week. Thanks to James Moffat, Peter Moffat, and Constance Brissenden. Once again, warm appreciation goes to my agent, Leona Trainer; my editor, Carolyn Bateman; and all the staff at Whitecap Books. Last but not least, a salute to my series' new "plot coach," Mark McLennan of the adventure company B.C. Extreme (www.bcextreme.bc.ca).

praise for *Raging River*

"I loved the book! It was so fantastic, I read it all in one sitting. An action-filled tale of adventure in the Canadian wilderness. These boys experience a dream adventure!"

— Scott Shipley, three-time Olympian, ten-time U.S. National Champion kayak racer, and author of *Every Crushing Stroke: The Book of Performance Kayaking*

"This book has it all — exciting outdoor adventure, depth of background on real outdoor sports and natural environments!"

— Jamie Boulding, British Columbia. Executive Director, Strathcona Lodge and Canadian Outdoor Leadership Training

"Wow! I'm breathless! I couldn't put *Raging River* down until the last sentence was consumed. The story is believable because it is written with a true understanding of river hydraulics and kayaking technique. I'm giving a copy to each of my four grandchildren!"

— Judy Harrison, retired publisher of *Canoe & Kayak Magazine*

"*Raging River* is an incredible story that completely captivated me. It made me feel I was living the adventure. If you like adventure, it's a must read."

— Tao Berman, three-time world record holder and Pre-Worlds Champion

"This is a great story with lots of twists and turns. It's a page-turner for paddlers and non-paddlers alike."

— Charlie Walbridge, author of the *American Canoe Association's River Safety Anthology*, and other books

"An adventure story that will captivate the imagination of every youth who loves the outdoors."

— Margaret Langford, three-time Olympian and member of the Canadian Whitewater Kayak Team

"I was lucky to find a passion for kayaking at an early age. *Raging River* captures the excitement and love for the sport that has kept me motivated to chase my dreams. This book really takes it to the extreme."

— David Ford, eleven-time Canadian National Champion in whitewater slalom kayaking, 1999 World Champion, three-time Olympian and eight-time World Cup medalist

Read the exciting first chapter from another book in this series

RAGING
RIVER

1   The Apprentice

Angry river water slapped at the cold walls of the canyon as Jake Evans pulled on the oars of his inflatable rubber raft. He was sweating to maneuver the stupid thing into a pool of calm water before taking on the last churning rapid. He turned his weary gaze to the jagged, mid-river boulder just downstream: a massive finger that rose defiantly from the river's depths.

"Devil's Finger," he muttered, shivering. Jake swiveled to study the dark clouds beginning to choke out what little light was left of this spring day and told himself that one more treacherous rapid wasn't a big deal after a full day's training.

He shivered again as he ran a hand down the rubbery neoprene of his wetsuit, the one he'd finally bought after saving a month's allowance and some of his weekend wages. It was adult-sized — a bit baggy for a fifteen-year-old — but he figured his lanky body came close enough to filling it. At least it kept out the brisk wind and icy waves. Jake breathed in the damp fog and smell of wet forest and sighed. A part of him wanted to climb out of the raft and curl up on a log to sleep. Another part wanted to light a stick of dynamite and toss it at Devil's Finger. That way, he'd blast two complicated paths through a rapid into one smooth cascade and a "yahoo!" sort of ride to the day's finish.

River raft guides, of course — even trainees like himself — weren't supposed to think like that. They were supposed to be totally into nature and challenge. And most days, Jake was. He just needed a quick injection of energy and courage right now to get around this ugly boulder and slalom neatly through the jumble of rocks and water below it. Then he could pull up full of confidence to where his boss, Nancy Sheppard, stood. He imagined his tall, lean, thirty-year-old supervisor stepping up to the raft to shake his hand, and instantly promoting him from trainee to junior guide.

Jake shrugged off his silly reverie and got ready to dip his oars back into the current. He would take the fork to the left of the evil finger, angle his raft from the riverbank to just above the boulder, then swivel into the long, foam-laced tongue of water that wrapped itself around the rock. Nancy, whose years of experience had earned her head-guide status at this adventure tour company in Chilliwack, British Columbia, Canada, had told him to steer left here at high water. He could see Nancy on the shore far below, a distant figure holding a rescue rope and standing beside a pile of trainees' rafts. He relaxed his grip. They'd made it; so would he.

With a surge of confidence, he plunged his oars into the current and whipped his craft around into the choppy whitewater. But as the raft shot out of its resting eddy, its front lifted too high on a surf wave and skidded sideways. Jake's pulse quickened as a downstream wall of gray water rose to cut off his view of the boulder. The canyon walls all around him began tilting at crazy angles. As his craft spun out of control toward the face of the finger, Jake shifted on his plank seat and dug his oars in harder to straighten out and avoid the blinding spray of water ricocheting off the stone's pocked face. Next, he launched himself into the front compartment and frantically pressed himself against the bottom of the boat, trying to force it down. It was the only way he could think of to stop the raft wrapping itself around the boulder like a dish-rag. The last thing he remembered was his shoulder smashing into the unyielding edge of Devil's Finger as the boat slid up against its left face, hesitated, and, with a shudder, twisted and folded over Jake's sinking body.

Nancy told him later that she'd never seen a raft spiral and fold quite like that. Nor had she ever seen an overturned, runaway raft pinball down a rapid so smoothly, picking its path intelligently, running on autopilot while its stunned driver remained temporarily trapped underneath.

What Jake did remember was this: Nancy and the trainees lifting him out of a frosty pool well below where he meant to end up. If that wasn't embarrassing enough, his next sight, as he sat crouched on the cold riverbank, was of Peter Montpetit, his childhood friend-turned-jerk. Peter, arms crossed and sneering down at him, was framed by half a dozen kayak racers attending an elite training camp just downstream of the rafters' take-out point. Jake hadn't yet made the Canadian whitewater kayak team this year and had missed this weekend's session for lack of money. Now here he was, washed up at their training camp with a bruised shoulder and torn wetsuit — a failed raft guide, staring up into a ring of superior faces.

"… And if he doesn't live," Peter was saying in his clear, booming voice, blond curls wagging, "I know for certain that his will provides for that wetsuit to be donated to my club in Seattle."

"*Seattle*," thought Jake wearily. Peter's father had nabbed a fancy job in the States a few years ago, and Peter had been able to join the U.S. kayak team because his dad was a U.S. citizen. The novelty of the situation still hadn't worn off, and Peter liked to lord his new credentials over his former Canadian teammates. Still, they didn't seem to mind, welcoming him back on his weekend visits to their kayak training site near Chilliwack, just north of Seattle over the U.S.–Canadian border.

"Back off," Jake responded as Nancy helped him to his feet. "I'm okay." He eyed the rocky shore and avoided the eyes of both the kayakers and his fellow raft-guide trainees. "Where's my raft?"

"The gang'll load it onto the bus trailer in a minute. It's in perfect condition, amazingly enough," Nancy replied. "The trainees and I did a merry chase after your raft, you know, but it wasn't until the kayakers joined in that we managed to pull it out. And there you were, floating comfortably alongside, one arm tucked into a side rope, hiding like Houdini. Kate has jogged back for the bus and here we all are."

Kate Johnston, Nancy's short, pudgy assistant, had gel-spiked hair and more energy than a hamster on an exercise wheel. She was helping with trainee evaluations today. Peter and the other racers, instead of moving off, hung around as Nancy continued. Jake felt a hot patch creep up his neck and into his face.

"Seriously, Jake, you made all the right decisions after you got turned around. You prevented a more dangerous splat against the upstream side of the boulder. We're not into losing a trainee or an expensive raft like that, right gang?" Nancy turned to the rest of the guide trainees — two girls, five guys, all older than Jake — who gave her a thumbs-up.

"Right!" they murmured.

"So, Jake, just another day in the life of a guide. You demonstrated good instincts and no doubt learned about the power needed to paddle across a flooding river. You'll make a good raft guide yet, but it's time to get you into dry clothes and call it a day. Especially since it's starting to rain." Turning to Peter and the rest of the kayakers, she added, "Thanks again for your help."

Peter separated himself from the group and sidled up to Jake. "Is the shoulder okay?" he asked, putting out a tentative hand to touch Jake's arm.

"It's bruised, that's all," said Jake, shrugging off Peter's touch. He'd seen his old friend shift from his hot-jock mode to concern in an eye blink a few too many times, and he wasn't taken in. "Won't stop me from hammering you next race." He hoped his grin didn't resemble a grimace.

"In your kayak or your raft?" Peter shot back. The Canadian team members guffawed on cue and pressed around Peter like groupies at a rock concert as the blond hotshot spun around and headed back to the kayak camp.

Jake gave the kayakers a mock salute with his good shoulder and followed Nancy's troop back to the raft company's old repainted school bus as raindrops turned into fat splatters. He shook his head as Nancy offered him a towel and fleece jacket, but accepted them once he was inside the bus. From a window, he watched Peter stuff his head of yellow curls — the ones the girls always fell for — into his gold-speckled helmet and lower himself smoothly into his tight-fitting kayak. Rain pelted down as the slalom racers maneuvered their smart boats neatly between poles hung on wires over the fast-moving river.

Of all the places to wash up, why at the kayakers' feet? Jake thought, burying his helmeted head in his hands. Many of them acted stuck-up around him, or maybe he just imagined it because they all had nicer boats than he did and they'd made the team and he hadn't yet. But Peter had definitely become a first-class creep. Jake raised his face and looked out the bus window just in time to see Peter form a perfect pirouette around a candy-striped slalom pole. Jake felt envy course through his shivering body and ooze out through holes in his rubber wetsuit boots. To Jake, Peter had it all: good looks, confidence, athletic talent — and money.

Only a few years earlier, the two had been insepara-ble. They'd grown up next door to each other, Jake's father an airplane mechanic and Peter's dad a float-plane pilot for logging camps. Then things had gone bad between Jake's mother and father, and Jake's father had packed his bags and left late one Saturday night after the worst fight ever. Jake could still hear the sound of a plate smashing on the tiled floor in the kitchen — and the unnatural quiet in the house after the front door had slammed. Jake's dad had disappeared without so much as a letter to his family since. That same month, Peter's dad had landed the job flying commercial airliners out of Seattle.

The two families' circumstances had diverged radically after that. In the end, Jake had lost not only a father, but his best buddy. Peter's more flush circumstances, along with his incredible success on the U.S. kayaking scene, had gone straight to his head. The two had lost contact for a while, and the friendship had died. Then, a few months ago, Peter had started showing up every weekend at Chilliwack's world-class training site, which was better than anything Seattle had, to boost his skills before U.S. Nationals. And the Canadian team members acted like he was a newly crowned king or something. Peter just didn't seem to see how arrogant he'd become and it really burned Jake's butt. Sometimes he wanted to pummel Peter blind; other times, he wanted to run away from the sound of Peter's exuberant voice and the shattered memories of good times they forced on him.

As far as Jake could tell, all Peter had to do these days was ask his parents, and they'd buy him a state-of-the-art kayak, a new wetsuit, even a trip to Costa Rica for pre-season training. Jake never asked his mother for money because he knew she didn't have much of it. Deadbeat Dads are hard to take to court when you can't find them. He was lucky to have an old race kayak to paddle and a weekend job that paid for rides to occasional races. Special coaching sessions were out of reach until he made the Canadian team and got some funding. Peter, on the other hand, probably had more weekly spending money than Jake could earn monthly between his paper route and weekends at the rafting company.

Jake had only just missed a slot on the Canadian team during a competition the previous weekend. It was a slot he wanted more than anything in the world. Lack of funds and his rafting job had kept him from attending this weekend's training, but he figured he could still clinch a berth at the next team trials. If he did, he'd be going to the National Championships less than two months away.

Even with the funding he'd get for making the Canadian team, he knew he'd have to save hard to afford the trip to Ontario for the Nationals. Jake's brow furrowed and he huddled into the hard, slick bus seat. Man, it was cold in here. How was he going to pay what he still owed for his wetsuit and save for Nationals at the same time? The wetsuit, of course, had been an essential purchase for his weekend rafting job — where he might still, despite today's big disaster, get promoted. Although too young to qualify as a full-fledged guide, Jake worked like a dog at the adventure tour company. He figured that was why Nancy encouraged him toward the junior guide slot, where he could guide in an emergency and develop boat-handling skills useful for when he turned eighteen. Besides, she'd told him he was the best cook in western Canada. It was a good thing Jake's mother had taught him a few things about making meals before taking her second, evening job. All those nights of making dinners for his younger sister had given him a useful skill for a raft company's Boy Friday. Jake knew Peter couldn't boil an egg if his life depended on it.

"Jake, what are you dreaming about?" Nancy called out as she leaped into the driver's seat and shut the front doors against the late afternoon shower. "Get out of those wet clothes before I have to assign the girls to strip you." The female trainees sitting up front giggled like sixth graders at recess, and deeper laughter and catcalls came from the guys, who were busy throwing the last of the oars and paddles into the muddy aisle of the bus. Jake obediently peeled his damp body out of the damaged wetsuit, after deciding he could mend the shoulder tear. Sometimes he felt an outsider in this group of older students, but he still liked their good-humored company and particularly enjoyed the after-work arm wrestling contests they got up to at headquarters. He could beat every one of the females except for Nancy, and one or two of the guys on a good day.

Jake watched Nancy move her lean but powerful frame down the bus aisle, checking gear. Guides and trainees fell silent as she passed. Though her weather-beaten face, tangle of black hair, and stern, dark eyes made her anything but good looking, Jake liked Nancy's relaxed manner. She had a quirky, deadpan humor off the river and she'd been raft guiding so long she was a legend in British Columbia. Jake often found himself wondering what it must be like to have guided that long — since the Dark Ages. Nancy Sheppard was simply the toughest, most perceptive person he knew. He liked working hard for her.

She also held the key to his two most immediate goals: the extra weekend work he had asked for so he could put money toward the Nationals, and the two weeks off he was counting on her giving him if he qualified to go. He hadn't asked Nancy about Nationals yet, of course. With Nancy, you didn't need to say much. Somehow, she always knew what was on your mind. That's probably why she had stood up for him in front of Peter and the team back there.

Jake squirmed again as he remembered looking up at that circle of kayakers' grins as he crawled out of the river. Next training camp, he'd be one of the kayakers, he vowed, not an unexpected, washed-up observer. And next weekend at team trials, he'd qualify for the team, whatever the slalom course had in store. It would be his last chance. He'd hardly registered this thought when he felt the bus take a sharp swerve, heard Nancy's piercing scream, and found his half-dressed body plunging off the bus seat. It slid heavily up the aisle until his head drove into the gear-shift box.

About the Author

Pam Withers has worked as an outdoor guide, journalist, editor, and associate publisher. A former associate editor of *Adventure Travel* magazine in New York City, she lives in Vancouver, British Columbia, Canada with her husband and teenaged son, where she enjoys skiing, snowboarding, and whitewater kayaking when she's not writing and editing books, or engaging in her other passion, public speaking.

Look for the next book in the *Take It to the Extreme* series, when Jake and Peter embark on the mountain biking adventure of their lives. For more information on the series, to write Pam, or to book her as a speaker, check out www.TakeItToTheExtreme.com